# THE THIEF'S GAMBIT

SARAH MÄKELÄ
TAVIN SØREN

KISSA PRESS LLC

# THE THIEF'S GAMBIT

EDGE OF OBLIVION, BOOK TWO

*A thief working for a local mob boss gambles everything...all for the chance to love his boss's daughter.*

Timothy Sands is an experienced thief with an old gambling debt. Working for the local mob brings him face to face with a supernatural threat unlike anything he's ever experienced. It'll take all of his skills to complete his assignment and keep his loved ones safe. But his greatest danger will be meeting the mob boss's daughter.

Letizia Prosdocimi is the only daughter of an influential crime boss. Her life forever changes when her father acquires a long-lost family heirloom. Not all is well since sinister events surround the amulet and her family. After being saved by the mysterious thief, she finds herself falling for him, but those who get too close to her usually wind up dead.

A shadowy entity threatens to tear apart everything Letizia and Timothy hold dear by feeding on the living and turning allies against them. Who can they trust? Only by working together will they have a chance to beat the odds...and let their love grow.

Sign up for Sarah's newsletter for her latest news, giveaways, excerpts, and much more!
http://bit.ly/SarahMakelaNewsletter

Editor: EB Editorial Services

Cover Artist: A.C. James

ISBN-13: 978-1-942873-03-7

# 1

## TIMOTHY

Vibrations on the nightstand shattered the last few moments of my sleep. The dark night peered from the curtains. I cursed under my breath. There was little point in fighting to reunite with sleep's warm embrace. London didn't sleep, and neither did those who required my services.

I picked up my mobile phone and cleared my throat before answering, despite the fact it would do little to hide my grogginess from the caller. An unknown number popped up on the screen, but only a handful of people would ring me at this ungodly hour. A grimace spread across my lips as I answered the call.

"Good evening, Timothy. We have another assignment for you, one that requires your immediate attention. If you take this, we might be willing to overlook your lack of payment last week." The man's dry, lackluster voice had a crisp accent. He'd never given me his name, never shared many details about my assignments either. He merely brought them to my attention and made sure I paid my debt.

Hallmarks of the city's darker elements were all too obvious, but what could I do? I owed the local mob boss more than I cared to admit. My old gambling habit had my back pressed tight against the wall, and I still paid for my wild and reckless youth.

"I'll do it," I replied, and the unnamed man on the other end of the line hung up.

Now I'd log into various websites and search for public postings in the adult and other less savory sections. Missed connections were very popular with my clients, but risky assignments were something my clientele didn't want to be associated with. Probably had something to do with recent notices about various three-letter agencies cracking down on this type of communication, driving everyone back to using older, tried and true methods.

I grabbed a cup of coffee before firing up my laptop. When the computer finished loading, I opened the browser and set off to find details on my newest job. It didn't take long to locate the assignment.

An old lady wanted the company of a young man who had previously helped her in a museum. Apparently, she had been quite taken by the gentleman's knowledge of the exhibit, especially the old Italian necklace that had been on display.

I chuckled to myself, still shaking the last vestiges of sleep from my mind. So, this 'old lady' wanted 'help' with the necklace, huh? Not very subtle, but if it made my clients feel more at ease that I'd understand the job... However, I hoped the person who created the listing would be less cheesy next time.

I flagged the posting as fraud and logged out.

My client would get an email notice about being flagged, the sign I had taken the job. No one would be the wiser. No face-to-face meetings to discuss things before-

hand, strict anonymity, and, most importantly, full deni-
ability.

A generalized search on the museums in the area
revealed only one matching entry based on the item's
description, the Royal Museum of Art. *Good.* At least there
would be no confusion about what the client wanted.
Nothing frustrated me more than stealing the wrong item. A
mistake I tried my hardest not to make ever again.

On second thought, I rang my brother Sam. It nearly
went to voicemail when he answered with his typical gruff
tone. "What is it?"

A slight sting of jealousy tightened my chest. He'd been
up enjoying his Saturday night, but I no longer had that
luxury.

"Hey, Sam. I just wanted to let you know I got another
job. My client wants an Italian artifact appraised as soon as
possible. Seems he can't wait until tomorrow. It looks like I
won't be making it to breakfast. Can I catch up with you
another time?" I hoped he'd buy into my bullshit about the
job. He respected what he thought I did. If he only knew...

Missing our weekly get-together bothered me. Our time
to catch up on one another's lives started when I'd moved
out on my own. Meeting with him meant a lot to me.

"Seriously, mate? You're always hunting for one piece of
art or another. Some things are better left buried." He
sighed in my ear. "But you've got a job to do. Just be careful.
That major explosion wasn't long ago, and I'm afraid for our
country. The MI6 agent still hasn't been found. He's most
likely dead, or maybe terrorists abducted him. If it can
happen to someone like that..." Sam cleared his throat.
"Anyway, you can pick up the check next week." His dry
humor almost managed to hide his disappointment, but I
knew him too well.

"Fair, I'll pay for breakfast next time." I ran a hand through my sleep-tousled hair. "Don't worry about me. I might not be MI6, but I know how to take care of myself." My skills had kept me alive while dealing with the mob, but my brother didn't need to know that. "As for my job, I'll slow down when I can. I promise."

"Right. Text me if things change." He let out a loud yawn.

Unfortunately, I doubted they would. "Get some sleep." I ended the call and set my mobile on the desk.

Sam didn't know about my nightly excursions. The less he knew about the darker side of the world, the better. Our parents had died when we were young. Night terrors and mental issues plagued Sam ever since. If he knew I was working on the other side of the law, he'd lose it.

The explosion that took place a few weeks ago returned to my mind.

While driving home after lunch, a building ahead of us had exploded into flames. I barely had a chance to slam on the brakes. Debris plastered the windshield, putting several cracks in it. Sam went white with shock, shaking uncontrollably and refusing to speak with anyone for the rest of the day. It had broken me to see him like that.

I couldn't let him suffer again, but if I didn't do my job, the mob might come after him. They knew he was my one weakness. I shelved the uncomfortable thoughts and packed a few supplies into my backpack.

My old, reliable Toyota sputtered as the engine came to life. Most of my neighbors were used to my odd hours, so this departure would be ignored as another student partying late into the night. Sometimes I was glad to live near a university.

The motorway was empty at this time of night, but a

dense fog rolling through the area forced me to slow down. An annoyance maybe, but I embraced its presence. It reminded me just how much we didn't see of the real world.

I pulled into an unlit corner of the museum's parking lot. The street lamps did nothing to penetrate the fog, which would help me make a clean escape. The museum grounds had a few exhibits tied to the Italian Renaissance, including a collection of marble statues. They were obviously replicas, but their finely sculpted silhouettes managed to portray an air of authenticity.

Stalking through the mists was invigorating, and I relished the moment. The fog would help conceal my shape from any cameras and guards on the property, but it was better to be safe. I slid into my gear and donned a gray and white leather mask. It was old school, but at least I didn't need to worry about it falling off if I had to sprint through the trees to my car.

Sweeping trails of light shone across the yard from me. Instead of illuminating anything, the cone of light likely made it impossible for the guards to see anything in the fog.

*Typical. Guess that's why I'm the thief.*

Along the side of the building, I located a set of utility boxes high on the wall. They might have been difficult to reach without a ladder, and impossible for an ordinary thief to exploit. That was why my employers enjoyed my services. I was far from common.

I set my backpack down and began assembling my composite bow. As I threaded the thick wire through the pulleys with practiced motions, I scanned my surroundings to make sure the guards weren't close, then prepared my arrows. Two of them acted like grappling hooks with ropes trailing from them. The ends of the shafts were bent at a backward angle and reinforced with hooks intended to catch small sharks.

I constructed the remaining broadhead arrows as well. Typically, I used them to disable cameras from a distance. I could also use the deadly arrowheads against a guard in an emergency, though the very notion turned my stomach. So far, I hadn't needed to do so, but one thing was certain—I refused to be jailed.

I shot the first arrow just beyond the edge of the roof, catching it on the bricks. As soon as I found a proper hold, I pulled myself up to the utility box and fastened the rope. My safety belt carried my weight, allowing hands-free access to the lock on the small, gray box.

The lock didn't stand a chance. With a couple wiggles of my lock picks, it clicked open. The inside housed older cabling from an outdated system. It connected the museum's alarm system to a black modem and onward to a standard phone line. No modern wireless transmitters, no backup cabling, or anything else that might pose a problem. The lack of secondary switching and circuitry made it evident that security was an afterthought to the museum.

*Maybe they need to receive an anonymous tip about this.*

Cutting the phone line or any components would raise the alarm, so I shorted the central circuit. The signal the modem regularly sent out would remain intact, but it bought me a few extra minutes before the authorities knew anything was wrong. By that time, I hoped to be gone.

Once the alarm was dealt with, I silently dropped to the ground. I gathered my supplies and the arrows, shoving everything into my backpack. My distraction nearly brought me face to face with a patrolling guard.

The cone of light helped me to locate him, and I swiftly ducked behind a nearby statue for cover. Effectively blind, the guard strolled by a couple feet from me and was none the wiser. Sweat beaded on my forehead.

*Everything's fine. It'll all work out.*

A small smile tugged at the corners of my lips as I followed him inside. *Here's my chance.* No need to break windows or leave any trace of my presence. My padded boots hushed my steps.

As the guard made his way through the door, I waited until the last moment to block it from closing behind him. The guard, sloppy as ever, didn't bother verifying whether the door snapped shut. As long as his suspicion wasn't stirred, he could remain in his world of monotony, and I had no intention of breaking that illusion.

Tracking the security guard's clomping footsteps across the floor was easy. I kept my distance, inching deeper into the museum. Two other guards sat at the front desk more focused on discussing last night's Manchester United match than keeping the priceless objects on display safe.

Then again, most of the artifacts were wired to alarms, and we were in a busy city with CCTV cameras everywhere. Anyone stupid enough to steal something would likely be caught. I took my time scanning the open hall with its small signs pointing to the different exhibits.

As I stalked through the corridors toward the Italian Renaissance exhibition with its lavish paintings and sketches by the old grandmasters, I saw my target. A necklace adorned with glittering rubies rested on a soft satin display in its glass case. None of the guards were close by, no cameras pointed this way, and no visible wires seemed to track the item. And yet something about it was peculiar.

If I didn't focus, I found my mind wandering from the necklace, as if it wasn't worthy of my time. *Rubbish.* I fetched my tools to open the case. Even so, my thoughts kept returning to my brother's warning of things better left buried. Sam had never said anything like that before. Should I be careful? With an effort of will, I shook away those thoughts and zeroed my focus on cracking open the case.

Using a set of lenses, I checked for the most obvious alarms that might be in the case and found none. It didn't feel right. Why leave the necklace here with no visible protection? It seemed like a setup. Still, I had to retrieve the artifact to fulfill my task.

I took a deep breath then let it out. The mob would come after my brother and me if I didn't do this. My payment was well overdue and my debt so high I couldn't chicken out now. The decision had been made for me.

I slid the necklace into a cushioned satchel as a surge of electricity raced up my arm. The jolt caused me to nearly drop the amulet. Uneasy, I shoved it into the inside pocket of my jacket. Something brushed against my chest, as if the necklace had shifted. As if it was alive. No, I refused to believe that. My mind had to be playing tricks on me.

A strange sense of wrongness overwhelmed me. I had to get out of here. The sooner I delivered this necklace, the better. I could ask questions later.

Before I could take five steps, I heard the muffled moan.

A mummified corpse with a large headpiece smashed into the glass beside me. It struggled to free itself from its case in the Egyptian section. My heart leapt into my throat.

*What the hell is going on? Mummies don't move on their own!*

Adrenaline surged through my veins, and my reflexes kicked in. I'd be damned if I let that thing touch me.

*Time to go on the offensive.*

I pulled out my knife then darted to the case. I plunged

the blade into the mummy's eye socket, half-expecting blood to start gushing out. Instead, the body went limp. Within seconds, it shook and flailed its arms again.

*Bloody hell. Moving on!*

I slid my backpack on and ran toward the door where I'd come in. The dead should stay dead. The chances of the museum using animatronics like that was very low. Besides, the movements were so fluid. No animatronics could behave like that. Whatever was happening here could continue to do so without my presence.

*Here's a cursed talisman for you, sir. Good day!*

At that moment, one of the guards paused in the doorway. His widened eyes darted from me wielding a knife to the mummy thrashing around in the case. The guard's surprise turned to horror. His frozen stance saved me. Had his reaction time been a moment sooner, he might've been able to radio for help.

I punched him hard in the face then darted past. As I ran through the corridors of the museum, glass started shattering all around me. The security guards at the front desk were frantically radioing their friend as I passed them.

Hopefully, the guards would run instead of facing whatever those things were. Mummies, zombies, the undead? Who the hell cared so long as I didn't end up as their snack? Behind me, surprised screams reverberated off the walls. The guards must've met the mummies. Ripping and crunching sounds churned nausea in my gut. They fared as well as I'd feared.

*Damn.*

I shoved the exit door open and welcomed the mists that drifted through the museum's grounds ahead of me. At least it might hide me if those *things* hunted by sight. The sound of heavy footsteps and breaking windows told me the creatures were already after me. Could I outrun them? It didn't seem likely. If I couldn't, I needed to change tactics.

As I sprinted away from the building, I sheathed my knife and grabbed the bow from my back instead. I let loose an arrow where I thought the closest opponent would be. A satisfying *thunk* followed as the shaft sank into old flesh. I hoped it would be enough to stop it in its tracks.

Closing my eyes for a few heartbeats, I listened to the sounds around me.

The ancient monsters had outmaneuvered me, blocking my escape to the parking lot. Hiding their shapes from sight, they seemed to mock and toy with me. This was going to get ugly. Three sets of hobbling footsteps rustled from behind one of the tall Renaissance statues. They were probably grouping together, preparing for an attack.

A smile curved my lips as I pulled the string back on my bow. Low tech but utterly reliable, the modern composite bow carried enough stopping power to handle anything that walked on two legs. The weight of it in my arms was reassuring.

The previous corpse hadn't moved yet, which relaxed me a little more. Maybe the creatures wouldn't keep coming at me indefinitely.

The howl of a hunt carried through the fog. They were going to pounce, and soon. Five pairs of unsteady feet shuffled toward me from the dark mist, as if their primitive minds thought the lack of line of sight hindered me. If anything, it gave me an edge.

I let loose another arrow. Even before I heard it *thunk* into the target, I had two more sailing toward them. Their assault paused a moment before the two remaining horrors pushed forward and ran at me.

They were too close for my bow, so I tossed it onto my

back again. I took off toward the tree line. The shadows would likely give me a greater edge over them.

The creatures stopped and audibly sniffed the air, as if catching my scent. They reminded me more of ghouls than zombies. From what I'd seen in old horror films, zombies were utterly mindless. These things worked together.

They released another howling shriek as they headed my way. The one on the right raced toward me, faster than her companion. A female. The realization struck me even as I prepared for what was to come. I pulled a short sword from my backpack as first a shambling hand then the tip of a nose became visible through the thick fog. When I saw the shorter mummy's hollow eyes, I pounced.

With trained reflexes, I beheaded the female corpse running at me and spun away from the heavier male. Thankful for the sword in my hand, I pulled away from the remaining ghoul. A hungry growl of denial ripped through the mist as the creature's bloodlust fueled its shambling steps.

My right hand gripped the sword's hilt, but I still didn't feel safe here. My left hand moved to the knife at the small of my back. There wasn't much time. I could sever its limbs, but if its head remained, it might still be a threat.

If this was the only way back to my brother, then so be it. I could not—would not—allow some rotting undead to tear me apart. My debt was ever closer to being paid off, and I longed for the day when I didn't have to hide who I was from my brother. I wanted to be a respectable man again, one who deserved his admiration.

With a grim determination, I pulled the knife free from its sheath and took a step forward.

The ghoul froze in its tracks and went silent, the sound of nocturnal activity dying with it, until the museum grounds were so quiet you could hear a pin drop. The hair on the back of my neck stood on end. This wasn't supposed to happen. Primal predators usually didn't change strategies, especially after smelling blood.

Something else was here. Something powerful enough to make an undead calm down in either reverence or fear.

A soft crackle came from the trees surrounding the museum. Something slithered along the grass almost as softly as I did. The occasional snapping of branches was the only thing that betrayed my new target's movements. I took a tentative step back, then another as the intruder quietly wound its way toward the three bodies I'd dropped with arrows.

Soft, rumbling growls echoed from the middle of the road as the ghoul became increasingly agitated.

The sound built up to a howl that was cut short with a loud thump. The mist swirled lazily as something massive moved with speed. Past the thinning fog, I saw the outline of my opponent and froze. I dismissed the remaining ghoul. It wouldn't survive the next hit from that thing anyway.

I took careful steps backward, keeping the real predator of the woods in my line of sight. The padded footwear was a godsend. I didn't have firepower strong enough to bring down what seemed like a possessed tree. This wasn't part of the deal I'd made. While I appreciated the chance to reduce my debt to the mob, my life was worth more than dying at the hand of something out of a roleplaying monster manual.

Scanning the mist, I stalked along a dirt path toward my car. Other jobs could help pay off the debt I owed. Right now, I needed to make it out in one piece. There was another loud crash as the tree swatted the ghoul again. While it was slow, the strength behind its punch was more than enough to make the ground shake.

I reached the parking lot and sighed in relief. I waited there for a few seconds, listening to the strange noises that filled the night. The slaughter wasn't far away, but there should have been animals close by. Birds and squirrels normally had enough sense to vacate a dangerous area, but insects tended to care less. Instead, everything was dead quiet, as if I was alone in some alien world without any sign of life.

Then I heard it, a soft crack of timber. Easily dismissible during any other time. That crack of wood was the scariest sound I could think of right now. No animals, no wind, and no machinery were nearby. Even so, there it was. It repeated a few times, but the line of other trees made it impossible to place its location accurately.

The rustling of leaves behind me was the only warning I had. Rolling forward, I barely missed the huge branch that swatted against a tree trunk close to me. Had I been standing, I might be soft mush between the cracked tree and the possessed one. It smelled like rotting wood, and the earlier impact it had with the ghoul hadn't helped its scent.

The branch flexed as if invisible muscles tensed within the old oaken tree. There was no chance of cutting through its branches with my weapons, but I had to do something. If I just ran away, who knew how many people this thing would kill?

*Bloody hell.*

I turned and bolted from the spot, making a beeline for my car. The old Toyota had seen enough damage in its lifetime, but I hoped it would start in one go this time. I picked up my pace. The more distance I put between me and the haunted tree, the more time I had to coax the old car into action. Even as I grabbed the handle of the driver's door, soft whispers of leaves somewhere behind me filled the air. *Keys, door, engine.* My mind raced with the need to act as I yanked open the door and hopped in. I turned the key in the ignition. Once, twice, but no luck.

After the second turn, I glanced toward the museum's grounds to see sweeping tendrils of branches and tree roots. They snaked across the parking lot toward me. Here and there, a crack of wood was followed by a sudden lurch as tendrils came ever closer. The thing was using its branches for speed. I tried the ignition one last time before everything went silent. The rattling of leaves had stopped.

*Shite!* I bolted from the car.

Even as I raced away, air rushed behind me, nearly knocking me to the ground. With a massive thump and bang, the once reliable Toyota Corolla was now a heap of rubbish.

The tree branch tried to pull away from the bent metal frame, but it seemed to have trouble worming its way from the remains of my car.

A devious thought hit me, and I grabbed my bow. With a quick pull, I shot one of the broadheads into the gas tank, breaching the side of the wreck. As its last service to my family, that car would save my arse one final time. I sent another two arrows in, further penetrating the ruined car.

As if sensing something was off, the tree redoubled its efforts, but it only managed to pull the entire car up with it. A stream of gasoline poured from the car's tank, spreading around the parking lot. It continued to spill the sloshing liquid over the demon tree.

I grabbed a lighter from my pocket and ignited the stream of volatile fuel. The streak of fire rapidly spread, tearing through the ebbing fog as it hungrily immolated the tree. An unnatural howl, deep enough to make my bones vibrate, radiated from the massive beast.

The scream made me smile. I might've lost my faithful car and almost died fighting that thing. But I was still alive. There'd better be a bonus with this assignment. Besides, if the mob wanted me to continue working, I needed a new car.

## 2

## LETIZIA

The grand mansion's halls were packed with guests as my father hosted yet another charity event. A smile was plastered on my face as I mingled, saying a few words here and there to a select few guests. My primary focus was returning to my room. These functions always made me a little uncomfortable, and I wanted nothing more than to escape. Guests conversed about local politics around me, but I had no illusions of who these businessmen and women were and what they did.

Most of them were barely more legal in their business practices than my father. It made no difference if one ruled by financial means while another ruled with strength. Financial sharks, shady CEOs, and corrupt local politicians roamed with other criminals of the city. Sure, they held a 'respectable' profession that they showed the public, but each of them wore their true colors tonight. It was an evening of business and platitudes, after all.

A shiver chased down my spine, and I continued the trek to my bedroom.

Things within the family had changed since the days of

old. Technology that some thought would chase us underground to hide our illicit activities had become integral to day-to-day operations. Business analysis, meticulous bookkeeping, and online tracking of goods and services were now essentials. I'd argue that they were even more important than the enforcers my father hired to keep his interests safe.

While I wasn't happy with what my father did, it was all I'd known growing up. As much as I wanted to do something different with my life, continuing the family's business was expected of me. I didn't have many other options.

Musings about my fate gnawed at my mind as I walked toward the library. Of the forty-three rooms in the mansion, this one was by far my favorite. My family was closer to our roots than ever before. Familial artifacts, books containing our history, and priceless works of art kept us anchored. They reminded us of what our family had faced throughout the years. We'd been brought devastatingly low, only to rise again. My father swore that circle of resurrection would not be repeated during his lifetime.

Two beefy men in black suits guarded the library doors, causing me to slow my pace. We had company, but that wasn't rare. I peeked inside to see my strong father. His gray hair did nothing to disprove the power at his disposal. Other families used brute force and coercion, but Papa always behaved like a strong-willed businessman. The kind you'd want to make a deal with.

A younger man with dark hair around my age stood before him with his arms at his sides. He looked like he'd been in a fight. His jacket was torn and grass stains covered his black jeans.

"Letizia, come. I have something to show you." My father waved me into the library to join him. The bright smile on his face was genuine, which surprised me. I loved seeing my father happy, but the young man obviously had nothing to do with the charity event. No, this had to be the less legal side of his business.

With a casual smile, I walked between the guards. Two more men stood watch in the office. Usually, my father's guards stayed out of sight, but right now, they didn't bother to hide their intimidating presence.

*Definitely business.* I rounded the mahogany desk to my father's side. "Good evening, Papa. The charity fundraiser is going well. What did you want to show me?"

"Good, I'm glad to hear it." He nodded his approval. "After many years of searching, I have finally acquired something that once belonged to our family generations ago. My grandmother used to speak of a black sheep in our family, an aunt of hers who returned to the old ways before *stregoneria* was brought into the open. And unlike *stregoneria*, my grandmother said her aunt found something older to study and use before she left Italy. It took a fair amount of determination and wit to track down clues, but my men finally located it. And now, it is where it belongs." Pride brightened my father's face. With a wave of his hand, he beckoned the dark-haired man toward us.

The man pulled a cloth pouch from the inside of his jacket. His movements were careful and controlled. Was he afraid he'd be killed otherwise? He set an amulet on Papa's desk that looked to be a golden half-moon with an intricate scroll and ancient text around its edges.

My gaze lifted to study the man. His face was sharp and angular with stubble lining his jaw. An aura of danger floated around him, and my heart skipped a beat as his green-eyed gaze met mine.

"Gorgeous, Mr. Sands. Consider me impressed." My

father slid on a pair of white cotton gloves to investigate the necklace further. If what he said was true, this was a very important find. It would make an excellent addition to our collection. My father certainly seemed to appreciate the amulet.

Then again, I was charmed by something...or someone else, too.

*Stop it. Your father is with the mob, and that guy screams trouble. You're not thinking straight.*

Heat warmed my face, and I bunched my hands into fists before releasing them. *Stop acting like a love-struck teenager.* I focused on my father once more. He brought the amulet closer to his face, using a magnifying glass to likely make out the finer details of the text.

"It appears to be the genuine artifact. For someone as skilled as yourself, I'm pleased you've chosen to be in my employment. You'll receive compensation through the usual channels. As for your destroyed car, a new vehicle will be provided. Don't screw it up." My father's strict tone suggested the man should be grateful for the arrangement.

Tension twitched in the young man's jaw before he nodded. Had he really *chosen* to be employed by my father? Something about that didn't ring true from their interactions.

"Of course, sir. Please be careful with it. My car... Something strange happened when I retrieved your heirloom. I —" My father dismissed Mr. Sands's words with a wave of his hand.

"I'm well aware of what you told my associate when you were retrieved. Consider me a skeptic. Just be happy the assignment was successfully completed. Someone will be in touch soon enough with a new job. You may leave now, Mr. Sands." Something in my father's face changed. Annoyance roughened his voice, and he shot me a stern look. Had he noticed me eyeing his thief?

I lowered my gaze to his desk, pretending to be bored by the exchange.

"Fred, place this in the new display case."

My father trusted his druggy friend more than he did me with our family's amulet? Something like jealousy burned in my stomach. *Whatever.*

Fred stumbled as he walked toward the desk, and I fought not to roll my eyes. Why did my father keep him on his payroll? Sooner or later, he'd be too drugged or drunk to protect my father...or worse. When that happened, we'd all pay the price for his addiction.

My father ignored him. "Do you think the guests were entertained by my speech?" he asked me. His charm worked wonderfully on both the wealthy and the criminal citizens of the city. They were happy to support the privately-owned mental asylum that had fallen on hard times.

"Everyone I spoke with thought your speech was brilliantly said, Papa. You were excellent."

The recent influx of addicts and mentally disturbed people had strained them far more than they'd imagined, especially with the recent closure of a government-operated facility nearby. Maybe the attendees were concerned for the wellbeing of those less fortunate, but part of me suspected most wanted to impress their peers with the size of their wallets. *Who knows?* They could've been hoping to repay the world for the damage they'd caused over the years.

"The one with a guilty conscience will always pay the best," my father had said before the event started. Sure enough, the local politicians were the first ones to write checks.

"I'm glad to hear that. It's important to choose your

words carefully and make sure they are respected." He patted my hand. That was a point he'd made many times throughout the years.

"I know, Papa. I've always done my best to make you proud."

Fred stumbled again, grabbing a nearby bookcase for support. Everyone turned to him in surprise.

My father took a step toward him, his gaze focused on the amulet as if trying to see if Fred's meaty, bare hand had damaged the priceless family artifact in any way. "Is everything okay, Fred? I'm glad you didn't drop it. I'd have your hide if you did." My father chuckled, but I imagined his words weren't far from the truth.

A loud hiss escaped Fred's throat as he turned to face us. His eyes rolled back, and his expression went blank. He moved in abrupt, jerky motions, and his hand went for the gun in his shoulder holster. "Run," Fred said, his voice hoarse with strain. The two bodyguards rushed for my father, blocking any line of fire to him.

My body froze in terror as I realized how unprotected I was. The fourth man who had guarded the door remained near the library's entrance.

"Don't even touch your gun!" one of the guards shouted.

The other man standing in front of my father barked, "I will shoot you, Fred! No one wants that."

"What are you doing, man? Listen to us!"

But their commands had no effect on him.

Something changed in Fred's face, and it almost looked like he gave in to some internal struggle. Blood spurted from his nose, and his actions suddenly became fluid, as if something else controlled him now. One minute, his hand was in his jacket, and the next, he had his pistol pointed at me. My father tried to shove one of his bodyguards in front of me, but they didn't budge. To them, I'd be a casualty to mourn later.

Tears welled in my eyes. So, this was it...

Before I could comprehend what was happening, I was thrown from my feet and rolling behind a sturdy bookcase in a currently unlit section of the library. Silenced shots pierced the books above me as my momentum kept me spinning.

The sound of gunfire broke out in the library. Anyone thinking a silenced pistol made no noise had never heard one being used. Forget Hollywood. Part of me wondered if my father's guests were already calling the cops, but no one in their right mind would do that. Not here.

The smell of sweat and musk shifted my gaze to my savior who hovered over me. The rip in his jacket gave away his identity before I could make out his features. His closeness was soothing, and the feeling of his hands around my waist warmed my insides. Part of me wanted to stay there with him, but I needed to make sure my father was okay.

More gunshots broke the silence, and I winced at each of them.

"Letizia, are you okay?" My father's voice carried from the central section of the library where his desk stood. For the first time in forever, I heard traces of fear in his voice.

The weight of my protector's body over mine held me in place. I moved a little, and he backed off as if he only now noticed our precarious position. "I'm fine. Are you all right?"

The fact he'd spoken had to be proof he was, but someone would be dead. I had my suspicions, but at least my family had remained intact. Mr. Sands helped me to my feet, and I adjusted my dress before peeking around the bookshelf to make sure it was safe. My gaze froze on the bloody results of the firefight.

I turned back to my savior, but he was gone. My head spun, nearly spilling me back to the floor. Instead, I leaned against the bookshelf, releasing a slow breath. His scent lingered around me, and an unmistakable desire to see him again clawed at my insides.

But the chances of that were likely slim to none now.

# 3

## TIMOTHY

My mind raced as I walked through my front door. The adrenaline rush my work usually gave me was addictive, but this job had been different. Ever since I liberated the damn necklace from the museum, an uneasy feeling clung to me. The creatures that had attacked me during my escape were mind-blowingly strange, sure. To then witness Alonzo Prosdocimi's guard suddenly go rogue? That event chilled me to the bone.

However, what unsettled me the most was something more familiar. Like a scent that comes out of nowhere, carrying with it a fleeting memory from a forgotten time. As much as I tried, I couldn't place it. During each incident, the gentle tugs pulled at me before chaos ensued, but I'd shoved the feelings aside as my sleep-deprived mind playing tricks on me.

Meeting Letizia Prosdocimi had thrown me off balance. Others spoke of how beautiful she was. They were right. From the second I saw her, I hadn't wanted to look away. Her stolen glances made me wonder if she felt something too, or maybe she couldn't stop staring at my disheveled appearance.

The moment the guard took aim at her, my instincts had kicked in. There'd been no hesitation, no concern for my own safety. Instead, I needed to keep her safe. Something those shitty guards her father hired hadn't bothered with. Hell, I shouldn't have lingered in the library, but my curiosity about her had overruled my common sense. Instead, I'd felt compelled to keep her safe.

I was a professional and didn't let myself daydream about my clients' daughters, especially ones who held thousands of quid in gambling debt over my head. But when her soft body pressed against mine, I hadn't wanted to let her go.

If I knew what was good for me, I wouldn't think about her anymore. My profession relied on reputation. Those who lost theirs wound up dead, and in a city where Alonzo Prosdocimi ruled the underworld, trying to woo Miss Prosdocimi would be tempting death.

Taking a sip of my beer, I tried to relax, but the evening's events continued to race through my head. Despite my best efforts, I couldn't sit still. Not surprising since I thought better on my feet. It was any wonder my flat's carpet was still in good shape.

*Focus.*

I drew in a deep breath.

With all the weird shite happening, maybe it was time to take a break from London. If I could get my head on straight and figure things out, life would be easier for everyone. My gaze drifted to the United States map on the refrigerator door. I trailed my finger over the state of Nevada. Las Vegas held nothing for me anymore, but an insidious desire to visit burned in my chest nonetheless.

An incoming text message chimed, breaking through my thoughts. I glanced at it and nearly dropped my phone. The number was associated with the Prosdocimi family business. It gave the time and location of a restaurant. Someone wanted to meet me tomorrow afternoon.

My mouth went dry. Had I somehow offended them?

I clenched my hands into fists and glanced back at the map. Vegas was looking better by the second. The sound of slot machines, cards being shuffled, and the clatter of dice against the table played in my head. Images of a life I'd tried to put behind me squeezed at my chest. Returning to my addiction was like a siren's call.

I took another long drink of beer, wishing I'd had something harder instead. Something that might numb the constant urge.

*Fuck.*

I slammed my fist against the map, then stalked out of the kitchen.

The television played the evening news, but I barely paid it any attention. Once the blinds to my bedroom were closed, I kicked the dirty clothes on the floor aside and emptied my backpack to check the gear. Whenever I did a job, I cleaned my tools. None of it was cheap, especially when I didn't earn a lot of money due to my debt.

Water had condensed on some of the items due to the heavy fog. My kit needed to remain in immaculate condition for my jobs to go smoothly. The last thing I needed was a set of lock picks to break or to have issues with my bow. Call me old-fashioned, but neither my bow nor blade made much noise. A gun would quickly give away my location.

Thoroughly cleaning my knife took the better half of an hour. With a whetstone and water, I painstakingly scrubbed off the dark specks of old blood and ancient flesh from the surface, then sharpened the blade until it was as good as new.

The television caught my attention as I picked up my bow.

A young, blonde reporter stood outside the museum telling of a strange heist that occurred earlier in the evening. She waved her hand toward the building as she pointed out how and where the thief might have entered the museum, indicating various access points up high and broken windows around the property.

*I'm not a bloody amateur, lady.*

Chuckling, I increased the telly's volume so I could listen while checking out the composite bow. Small leaves had found their way into the pulley system, and I cleaned it as the animated reporter moved on to say that police claimed it was one of the strangest heists they'd seen as the only items of value reported missing were several mummies that had been on display.

*What the shite?*

No one had noticed the Renaissance necklace's disappearance? My instincts nudged me again. Perhaps the police hadn't released that information yet. But didn't they see the damage done to the property? The glass from display cases breaking from the inside? The possessed tree in the parking lot?

Thankfully, Mr. Prosdocimi's flunky had towed the remains of my car from the parking lot, or the police might be knocking on my door with plenty of questions. At last, the reporter described how the security guards on the premises were likely in shock from their severe injuries.

Hell, all of them had witnessed something deeply terrifying. The men were sane to be haunted by the experience. I certainly was. And I didn't guard the dead for a living.

At least my description hadn't become public knowledge yet. However, they'd seen something. While people might shrug off stories of walking trees or reanimated corpses, a growing number of individuals online had begun connecting the dots that something wasn't quite right with our world anymore.

I wasn't sure what had happened, but my instincts had guided me in fighting the creatures. Freaking out wouldn't have helped anyone. I relied on the fighter within me who wanted to see his brother again. It didn't matter that a reanimated corpse or a possessed tree was coming at me. I'd deal with them.

I set the cleaned bow aside as I listened to the rest of the news. The media didn't have anything concrete about me or what had gone down. That was all I needed to know. Flicking off the television, I let my mind wander, content that I still had an advantage. My gaze went back to that damn map.

I'd gambled a lot of money to end up here.

When Sam and I were younger, our parents died in a car accident. Our grandparents had tried their best to give us a proper upbringing, but money was always tight for them. Things had been better with our parents. Life had been richer.

To compensate, I began working at a young age, both to help my grandparents and to have everything the other kids I hung around with did. But no matter how hard I worked, it was never enough. So, I supplemented my income in other... less savory ways, namely theft.

Paranoia always kept me looking over my shoulder. Most of the time, I wondered if everyone knew what I was doing, but somehow, I was never caught. Raising two young boys put a terrible stress on my grandfather.

One of my grandpa's military pals took the three of us on vacation to Las Vegas, the only vacation I'd had at that point in my life. From the moment we landed, I was hooked. At the age of twenty-one, the whole world felt like my playground.

My addiction started out innocently enough. Before long, I'd found myself sitting at blackjack tables with drinks being delivered by lovely, scantily clad young women. My head became completely fucked by the attention. With my parents dead and feeling invincible, I threw myself into gambling. I won a lot, and before long, I came up with a system. Enjoying myself wasn't part of the equation. I was there to win at any cost...and to pull myself from a life of soul-crushing mediocrity. The gambling continued even when we returned to London.

But my luck didn't last. The system I'd come up with didn't work. Pretty soon I gambled away my paychecks, the money I stole, and the savings my parents had left me. One day, I woke up so deeply in debt I didn't know which direction was up.

A couple of thugs strapped me to a chair and told me I had two options. Either pay off my debt by working for their boss or lose both of my kidneys. My pickpocketing skills hadn't gone unnoticed by the casino's staff.

It would've been so easy to end it all. Life had backed me into a corner, and I felt trapped.

Various flunkies pushed me to my limits. But I learned how to fight, pick locks under intense pressure, and hone my skills at theft. For better or worse, I had a knack for the job. If some rich snob skipped out on his bill, the casino tasked me with taking his fancy car or breaking into his vault.

Theft soon became more addictive than gambling. I enjoyed my job. A little too much, in fact, but I'd racked up so much debt nothing I did helped. Some days, the adrenaline rush was the only thing keeping me going. That, and the fact my brother needed me.

Without me, Sam would have no one. I couldn't surrender, not without a fight. I fully intended to make things right, but I couldn't get out yet.

Everything I did came around to bite me in the arse. The mob family likely knew I'd witnessed them gunning down one of their own, and I'd shown them I wasn't just a petty thief. The head of the family knew me now. I would be watched. If Alonzo suspected I had any intentions with his daughter, I'd most likely end up with her other suitors— beheaded and dumped in the Thames.

My thoughts circled back to Miss Prosdocimi, even though I had no business thinking of her. The red satin dress she'd worn had exposed her long legs and clung to her curves. She appeared every bit as confident as her father. Her hands gently rested on my chest while I'd pinned her to the library's floor. Her body pressed so close to mine I could've pretended she hadn't been shot at.

*That's enough, Tim. She's out of your league.*

Sunlight peeked between the curtains, and I groaned. There went any chance of me sleeping. My eyelids drooped as I looked around my flat. Exhaustion sank heavily upon my shoulders, and I became aware of just how tired I was. The adrenaline rush during a job was great, but when I finally made it to the other side, it left me weak and shaky.

I threw a frozen dinner into the microwave and rested my forehead against the kitchen counter. *Rob this, break in there, steal that. Pay off debt and never dream big. Bullshit.* I'd tasted the better side of life before everything came crashing down around me.

My life had been lived poorly and without control. Now control was all I had left. I'd die before giving that up for anyone or anything.

## 4

# LETIZIA

Thick, dark clouds loomed over the city carrying a promise of rain that never seemed to materialize. The entire day was bathed in gloom. Without a clock, it was difficult to know if time was actually passing.

Nervousness thrummed through me as I opened my bedroom door. Bribing one of my father's assistants to reach out to the thief who saved my life had been costly, but I didn't care. Every time I found myself unfocused, his piercing green gaze returned to my mind, along with that earthy, masculine scent. Was I making a mistake by asking him to meet?

No way. I needed to thank him for saving my life.

But maybe he was already seeing someone...like a girlfriend.

The lapse of concentration nearly sent me crashing into an antique Japanese table placed in the middle of a wide hallway. The guards seemed to be in their daily floor meeting, since not many were around. Good. If one of them followed me, it'd be disastrous.

I slowly progressed through the house, glad my father

hadn't installed those security cameras he'd talked about last year. If I told Papa I was heading into town, he'd assign a bodyguard or two to keep an eye on me. Any mention of meeting with Mr. Sands would end badly for us. I'd be placed under house arrest, he'd likely be dead, and my father would be draining a bottle of whiskey.

Part of me wanted to scream at my father for the way he treated me. It wouldn't change how things were, though. He saw me as his little girl, not a young woman who wanted to experience life—let alone date.

Ever since my mother had died, Papa lorded over me like I would break if not protected. I loved him, but the older I became, the more I felt like a prisoner in my own home. Those who wanted to know me better, even as mere friends, usually ended up moving away or having fatal 'accidents.' My father sometimes gave them a choice, and those who fled for their lives usually went unharmed.

Why couldn't he just accept that I needed my space and a life? I couldn't wait around anymore hoping one day he'd finally take a hint. It was time to do something about it.

I snuck downstairs to the common floors below and through the hallway leading toward the mansion's entrance. The heavy wooden doors to my father's study were firmly shut. Light escaped from the crack underneath. He'd labored over the artifact since receiving it last night. It was as if the necklace possessed him. He locked himself away in the study with a stack of books and a magnifying glass. At times, I swore I heard him talking to himself, as if clearing his thoughts like he did before his speeches. It was great having an item from our family's history returned to us, but I worried about what his obsession with the amulet was doing to him.

Even the bodyguards were on edge. They still cracked jokes and talked about sports, but they looked exhausted.

Footsteps up ahead brought me back to the present. I ducked into an alcove, wondering who it might be. Shift changes weren't this early, and I wasn't aware of any scheduled visits to my father at this hour.

The windows in the hall gave little light. Even so, the lanky build of the collector who helped my father trace some of the artifacts was recognizable. His odd gait gave him away, and the constant scent of peppermint seemed to follow him wherever he went. He held a hefty tome, and the man's attention was more on the door of the study than his surroundings. I was safe, for now. It was better if everyone thought I was still in my room.

Moving carefully, I made painstaking progress over the floor. The old wooden boards creaked and groaned due to old age. My father hadn't bothered paying anyone to fix the flooring, as it gave him a false sense of security. He'd tried to convince me that he would have a chance to react if someone walked past his study. It just meant I'd learned how to master that art as a rebellious teenager.

The collector closed the study doors. Here was my chance. Knowing the guards' routine, I dodged into the kitchen and waited for them to pass. Another short pause in the lobby as the men went for a coffee break. Their schedule shuffled every two weeks. Slowly, I headed for the outer doors, already tasting my freedom on the other side.

My little excursion almost ended before it even began as the front door slammed open. The mountain of a man with equally broad shoulders ducked under the doorframe. The scar slashed across his cheek sent a shiver down my spine. The thug—known as Little Boy—almost caught me. He strolled in as if he owned the place. The nearest window was rattled much like my confidence. A small, winding stair-case close to the entrance saved my hide, but the close encounter left my heart pounding.

*What is he doing here?* My father had him moved down south when he nearly killed one of our servants for acciden-tally spilling coffee on him.

As soon as Little Boy had left the lobby, I darted outside.

A few moments later, I walked down the road far enough from home to feel comfortable with calling a taxi. With each passing moment, I feared one of the staff would find me and call the guards to bring me home. By the time the car arrived, I'd almost given up hope and headed back indoors.

"Where to, miss?" The gentle voice of the driver startled me.

*Act normal. No one knows who you are.*

I gave him directions to a restaurant my family frequented. The staff knew my family, and they afforded us discretion whenever we ate there. The place acted as a neutral ground for negotiations between parties, so natu-rally, my father was a known face to many there. It hadn't been my first choice of location, but I could trust them not to spread the word of my meeting. The security of dining on neutral grounds made me feel safe enough.

After all, one never knew if anyone who wanted to sabo-tage my father's interests would try anything unsavory. It wasn't unheard of for other families to kidnap or kill those who opposed them. Powerful men usually had powerful enemies.

Giulia Stefani, the restaurant's hostess, smiled at me. "Hello, Miss Prosdocimi. Welcome back. Your table is ready for you." She glanced over my shoulder as if waiting for one or more escorts to appear. Her eyebrow lifted, and she led me to the table in the back that my family had specially reserved.

"Just you today?" she asked. She probably meant well, but the question made me uncomfortable. What if she decided to reach out to my father? Maybe I had made a mistake by coming here. "My acquaintance hasn't arrived yet, it seems. That's fine since he has five more minutes. I trust you will keep any knowledge of this dinner to yourself, Miss Stefani."

A broad smile curved her lips. "Of course, Miss Prosdocimi." Giving a nod, the slender hostess walked off, and I felt more at ease. I hoped she would be true to her word. I browsed the menu, even though I knew it well from coming here often with my father. Lamb, chicken, and beef were staples with various sauces and sides. While my father preferred the traditional, family-sized meals, I wondered where he stuffed those generous five-course meals.

No one I recognized was in view around the restaurant. Regardless, I couldn't shake the nervousness building up inside me. As one minute changed to the next, I wondered if my father had intercepted the message sent to my rescuer, or if Mr. Sands had gotten cold feet. My family did nothing to prevent the spread of rumors about what happened to those who dated me. In fact, part of me wondered if they spread them on purpose to deter any possible suitors.

I released a long sigh as I stared at the menu again. *Maybe he's stuck in traffic.* No matter what I did, the uneasiness wouldn't go away. Not used to being nervous, I let my hands fall into my napkin-covered lap, my palms damp with sweat.

An older couple at one of the tables rose from their chairs. The gentle touches they shared while helping the other with their coats spoke of love that still sparked between them. I couldn't help but smile at the thought of how amazing it must be to remain so close in old age. As they left the restaurant, I noticed my guest holding the door open for them.

Giulia spoke to him for a moment, then escorted him to my table. I sat up straighter. My heart pounded fiercely in my chest, and I drew in a few deep breaths. What was I thinking?

Jeans and a t-shirt that hugged his muscular chest and arms replaced the thick jacket and pants he'd worn before. His strong jawline and the slight smile on his lips nearly took my breath away. His piercing gaze seemed to see right through to my soul. He took controlled steps toward the table.

"Miss Prosdocimi?" He seemed caught off-guard but collected himself shortly. "Thank you for the invitation. May I join you?" he asked, standing beside a chair.

Giulia placed a menu on the table across from me and looked between us with humor in her eyes. She held the napkin for his lap in her hands, waiting for us.

"Be my guest," I said, trying to control my runaway thoughts. *Come on. You're not a teenager anymore.* "And please, call me Letizia."

When he finally sat, the hostess placed the napkin and smiled knowingly at me before leaving.

"Sorry for arriving late—"

"Don't worry about it." I waved my hand dismissively. His car had been totaled because of the job my father sent him on. While we had promised him a new car, it usually took some time to order new vehicles. We had to, of course, make sure the paperwork was legal enough to pass any checks. The poor guy probably had to take the bus to get here, or worse, the tube. "I wanted to thank you personally for saving my life and have a chance to get to know you a little." Thankfully my composure had returned.

He lifted his gaze to meet mine. "I'm happy you're okay. I'm sure anyone in my position would have done the same, Letizia." His deep voice sent a chill down my spine, but that small smile returned to his lips again. "I'm Timothy, by the way." He shrugged a shoulder as if rescuing damsels in distress was all part of the job.

"It's nice to meet you, Timothy." I laughed, feeling the tension surrounding our meeting slowly fade away.

Our server came to the table a few moments later, and we placed our orders.

Time flew by as we talked. The sound of his voice and his presence captured my full attention. The food tasted excellent, but all I could see was the man sitting across from me. We talked about our families, where we were from, and how we'd gotten to where we were.

My nervousness came crashing back through me as I saw movement from the corner of my eye. One of my father's assistants sat at a far table. Thankfully, he faced away from us. However, his presence drew my attention from the pleasant conversation. My handsome companion noticed the change of my focus quickly and stole a sideways glance at the man.

"Why is that guy making you uneasy?" Timothy asked, keeping his voice at the same conversational level we'd used up to that point.

"He works for my father," I whispered. "What?"

Timothy shook his head. "If you whisper, you'll draw attention. It's like yelling quietly. Everyone around who may be listening in will notice the dropped volume. Keep your voice level, and you'll disappear into the background. So, your father isn't aware of our dinner?" he asked, topping up our glasses with the last of the Sauvignon Blanc.

I nodded. He had an aptitude for this type of work, but his correction stung nevertheless. I was only trying to do what was right. The last thing I wanted was for him to be executed in a dark alley.

"That explains a lot. We should finish the meal and head out soon," Timothy said with a chuckle. Was he enjoying this? Was it a game to him? There was a twinkle in his eyes, and a genuine smile on his lips. "So, tell me more about the charity event that happened at your father's house."

The shift in our conversation surprised me.

"What can I say?" I took a sip of wine. "It's a pet project of my father's. When he heard that the privately-owned mental asylum had fallen on hard times, he decided to test his charm on his 'colleagues,' I guess. But I think he's also trying to make a difference."

"Aiding mental health is a noble cause regardless of your father's reasons."

My lips parted, and I blinked. It sounded like the topic hit close to home for him. I wanted to ask about his interest in the fundraiser, but I didn't have the heart to bring down the mood. If he wanted to tell me, he would. Right?

"Thank you. It was a successful night. The mental asylum will receive enough funds to keep going for a couple more years at least."

Timothy smiled. "I'm glad to hear it." His gaze slid over to my father's assistant who continued eating his meal alone. "Let's get out of here."

I pulled out enough money to cover the bill, then lifted my hand to get our server's attention. "I'd like to use the kitchen's exit."

The server nodded. "Of course, Miss Prosdocimi. I'm

happy to escort you out the back." The kitchen staff paid little attention to us as our server led the way. They were accustomed to not asking questions.

The alley we stepped out into was dark and cold, but we didn't need to worry about being spotted by my father's assistant. My shoulders relaxed ever so slightly. A gentle breeze picked up the scent of exotic spices as we passed a variety of stores. The smell made me crave something sweet.

We ducked into another alley to keep out of sight. The dirt and garbage in the alleyways did little to diminish my happy mood. Despite all the trouble, I enjoyed Timothy's company and the time we were spending together. I found myself partly relishing the mischievous getaway from the dinner and partly dreading getting caught.

"We can't go anywhere too public. Would you be offended if I invited you to my place?" Timothy asked.

I bit my lower lip but nodded after a moment. He was trustworthy. He'd saved my life after all. Besides, he had to know what could happen to him if he hurt me. Not that I'd be blameless. After all, I'd fled from my father and his guards to meet up with Timothy.

If we were caught, he wouldn't be the only one in trouble.

# 5

## TIMOTHY

We arrived at my flat just before eight o'clock. The taxi ride hadn't been cheap, but Letizia might've stood out too much on public transport. Besides, she'd taken care of the food. The least I could do was cover travel. To be safe, I'd asked the cabbie to drop us off a couple blocks away. As we walked, I remained aware of our surroundings in case we were followed, using the excuse that I needed fresh air after dinner.

The door to my flat creaked as I opened it. This was my first time having a woman here in quite a while. Work had taken over my life, so I rarely paid much attention to the fairer sex these days. Was bringing her here the right thing to do?

My place didn't have much furniture, mostly an older TV and a well-worn couch. Even the coffeemaker was an older model, not one of those fancy Keurig machines. Still, my belongings didn't matter. It was a place to rest my head while I worked to resolve my debt.

Pushing those thoughts away, I stepped aside to let her walk in first. "Welcome to my humble abode. It's not much, but it's home." I followed her inside and bolted the door behind us. Unlike her, I didn't have guards to protect me and mine.

"It's a nice place," Letizia said. The reserved tone in her voice didn't go over my head. She looked around a little before walking toward the couch. "Mind if I sit?" At my nod, she carefully seated herself.

The small smile playing on her lips made my heart pick up its pace. "Can I get you anything? Coffee, tea, or something stronger?"

"No, thank you. I'm okay."

I relaxed in an old recliner positioned beside the couch that had belonged to my grandfather. Silence stretched between us for a while, and I tapped my fingers against the leather arms trying to think of something to say. It wasn't my first time sitting near a beautiful woman. Bloody hell, we'd conversed easily enough at the restaurant.

"Crazy weather the other night, huh?"

Letizia frowned, as if she wasn't sure what I meant. "Weather...? Oh, the fog? It was different." She shifted on the worn couch cushions to face me. "Tell me more about yourself. How does someone like you decide to work for my father?"

My mouth went dry, and I glanced over at the map of the United States on my fridge. How much did she know about what her father did? Should I open up to her? "It's a long story."

"I have time."

"Listen, it's not a topic I like discussing." Would she leave if I opened up? If I didn't, she might come to worse conclusions, though. I sighed. "Okay, I used to have a gambling addiction." Probably still did, if I was honest. "Driving by the places I used to gamble is still hard. The need to play—and more importantly—to win constantly gnaws at me." I scrubbed my hands over my face. "Your father's men noticed my talent for theft, so instead of killing me, they brought me to him. He decided I was more useful working for him than dead in the Thames." I threw my arms wide. "That's probably why I'm still here." If her father knew I'd gone to dinner with her, chances were high that he'd rescind that decision.

Sadness and empathy mixed in her beautiful eyes. "I see. I'm sorry you landed on that side of my father's temper. It's good you've been able to overcome the addiction, even if the incentive likely wasn't pleasant." She leaned forward and placed her hand over mine. "He wasn't always this way, you know. My father used to be a kind man who put his family first. Unfortunately, that changed when my mother passed away." She shrugged a shoulder. "Now he's so protective of both me and his business. If anyone tries to 'do him wrong,' he strikes first and asks questions later."

"It happened, and I can't change that now. All I can do is try to make good decisions." That included working off my debt as quickly as possible. Her mother's death explained a few things. Losing my parents had changed my brother. Sometimes I barely recognized him anymore. "I'm sorry for your loss. I can relate a little. Ever since my parents died, my brother hasn't been the same."

This wasn't great first date material, but she made me feel like I could talk to her. That was new for me.

"I worry about him. There's a side to him that comes to the surface, and I feel powerless when it does. It's like he's a primal beast staring intently at his prey. Like he has his full attention on me and is looking for weakness. It freaks some people out and unnerves the rest. But he's not that kind of guy. He wouldn't hurt a fly." I told her before realizing what I'd said. Before I could clarify my thoughts, she nodded.

"My father is like that at times. He has a way about him when he collects himself. I could say he becomes very singular when that happens. People think they know my father, but unless they've been in the room when he gives his undivided attention to something, they've only seen the surface," she said, leaning closer toward me.

My eyes darted to the cut of her blouse, catching a glimpse of her alluring curves. My jaw went slack, and I lost my words. Before she caught my hungry stare, I dropped my gaze to our hands still touching on the chair's arm. Silence filled the room, but it wasn't heavy. A blush caressed her neck and cheeks as I closed the distance between us. I needed to be next to her.

Looking deeply in her eyes, I brushed my knuckles against her soft cheek. "I've never quite met anyone like you before, Letizia," I said, noticing that my voice trembled with emotion and anticipation.

Her eyes closed, and she leaned into my touch. "You know, Mr. Sands, my father would kill you without batting an eye, but I can't help myself. You've managed to steal my curiosity...and maybe my heart," she said with a teasing note in her voice as she leaned closer to me.

Our lips met in a gentle kiss. The caress of lips and tongue picked up their pace, and I laid her down on the couch. Her gentle curves fit perfectly against my muscular body. There was no rush, no need to do anything other than to make her happy. Breaking the kiss, I leaned back just enough to look her in the eyes. Her breasts pressed against my chest. I wanted to cup them in my hands and taste them, but I wouldn't proceed unless she was ready for this.

She tugged me closer and placed kisses over my face

while one of her hands slid toward the small of my back. "Timothy, I—" she said, her voice filled with the same need that burned inside me. We both wanted this. No, we needed it.

After I carried her to my bedroom, she removed my shirt, then teasingly took her time removing her own. The sight of her lovely lace-covered breasts took my breath away. How could I ever please someone so beautiful?

A sharp knock on the front door shattered the romantic mood. We looked at one another before panic hit us at the same time. *Please don't let it be her father.* With a few hushed motions, we smoothed out the bed, and she disappeared into the bathroom with her clothes. The lock faintly clicked in the door.

The knocks returned. This time they were more intense, more demanding, and I practically ran to the door, pulling my shirt on again. Better to let them in than have them break down the door.

Little Boy—a man so big he barely fit through the doorway—pushed in first, aggravation evident on his face. His flunkies followed him. Five men who looked like they barely shared five pounds of body fat between them gathered in my living room.

"What's this about?" I asked, trying to keep my voice level as I shut the door behind them.

Little Boy worked exclusively for Letizia's father in the enforcing branch. He was sent to those who missed one payment too many to encourage them to cough up their cash.

"Well, you really did it this time, Sands. You blew it," he said, stomping to my kitchen as if looking for something. Anger radiated through his voice. Something had him riled up. His flunkies' faces were sunken and a little hollow, each of them looking grim and ready to beat me to a pulp.

"Come on. You barged in here late at night without giving me a heads-up. What can I do for you?" I asked, looking at the men who were circling me now. Oh, shite. This wasn't going to end well.

A satisfied grunt came from the kitchen, and then the sound of the fridge door opening. "This isn't good at all," he said, then slammed the fridge shut. "You failed at your job." Part of me should have calmed down there and then. At least Alonzo was unaware of his daughter being here with me. That I knew of, at least. But this didn't make any sense.

"What do you mean I failed? I got the amulet, the police aren't knocking on your door, and my car is still totaled," I said, watching Little Boy roam around my apartment. Maybe I shouldn't have added the snarky comment, but I'd been promised a new car. How did they expect me to get their dirty work done for them? The London Underground?

"Boss says it's incomplete. You got the first half. Getting the second one should be a piece of cake, right? After all, I've heard all about how much of a big shot you are. He wants this done as soon as possible, so he's willing to toss in a small bonus. However, if a real professional completes it before you, the deal is off. All of it. No car, no payment. You follow?" His tone was as arrogant as his posture as he dropped onto my couch. The seat groaned under his weight, and I hoped to hell he wasn't about to break it.

"With a timetable like that, I need details, and I need them now." His words finally sunk in, and I shook my head. "Wait a minute. What do you mean the second half? I got him what was asked for. I did the work," I said, realizing how much might be at risk. If the family pulled my previous gig's money from the debt, I'd be in deep. Worse, I'd lose my reputation—no more jobs. The idea of going back to making a daily wage was horrible. I'd never be able to pay it all off, even if I had another lifetime or two to work.

"Not my problem. I'm here to make sure you get the message. And they're here in case you gave me any trouble." He waved at his flunkies and smirked. Little Boy placed his arms over the back of the couch, covering the entire length with his massive arms. "Oh, there's one more thing." He nodded to his boys.

Air burst from my lungs as the first man slammed his fist into me. The pain barely had a chance to register as the second man delivered another solid punch. The blows kept coming, but I rolled with them. My knees nearly gave out when they stepped away, but I remained upright.

"The boss appreciates the help with his daughter, but he wants to remind you of what happens to those who get too close to her." Little Boy heaved himself off the couch. "Little moths get burned, and I really like holding the candle." A smile spread across his lips as he said *candle*. There'd always been rumors about how he enjoyed torturing those who opposed the family. It seemed those tales were true.

The crew left the apartment. Each of them made a show of glaring at my door, as if to remind me that they knew where I lived. What was I going to do? Run away and pretend the debt didn't exist? If I tried to run at this point, I had a good idea what would happen. As the last man walked out, I quickly shut the door and bolted it. I really didn't want them coming back. Five minutes ago, I was having the time of my life. Now I was terrified.

*Shite.* I needed to step up my game and fast, especially with the added pressure of competition. But how? I didn't have any details on where to find the next piece. The artifact had looked complete when I'd held it. Bloody hell. I was dead in the water. There was little time to lose if the family was turning to other options, too. While I could get the piece without much attention, the more ruthless people in Alonzo's employment would bulldoze their way to victory just to get the head of the family to notice them.

Only now was my breathing returning to normal, but my stomach still ached from the assault. I glanced at the bedroom door. A pang of guilt tugged at my chest. If they'd caught her here, she'd have been in trouble, too. How would her father react to us together? I somehow doubted she'd get away with being scolded. I wanted her in my life, but maybe I needed to pull away first to save us both. Surely, she understood how close of a call that had been.

Still, if I didn't complete this job for her father, I was dead anyway. I had saved her life. Maybe she could help me with my current dilemma.

I knocked twice on the bedroom door before entering.

Letizia stood near the bathroom entrance with one of my smaller blades in her hand, ready to pounce. For a second, it looked like she was going to attack, but then she dropped the blade. "I take it they're gone?" she said, glancing past me to the living room. "What did they want?"

"Yeah, they've left for now. They wanted to encourage me to finish a job. Listen, you really should leave. I—"

"Leave? We were having a good time, and I enjoyed connecting with you during our conversation. What do you mean leave?" Each word became louder than the one before. She sat on the foot of my bed and slid on her heels.

"Wait, I didn't mean it like that. I was stupid, and I've risked too much having you here. You said it yourself, your dad would kill me if he knew about us." My words didn't seem to matter. I was digging my hole deeper. "Listen, I really liked our evening, but I can't have you here."

Letizia rolled her eyes. "Really? You're going to let my father stop you from exploring what we have? No, I was the stupid one for coming over. I just wanted to thank the man who had saved my life." She took her purse and headed for the door.

*Fucking hell.*

# 6

# LETIZIA

"Please, Letizia, wait. I'm sorry. I don't want you to get in trouble. If they caught you here…" Timothy's voice was thick with emotion, as if he couldn't bring himself to say the words. "I want us both to be safe."

He cared, and it felt really good.

Even if I didn't want to admit it, he was right. My father would kill him and likely lock me in my room and throw away the key if he knew we were together. The men I'd seen before were guys I met through school or at a bar. My father always warned me to stay away from the men he worked with, and it'd been easy. None of them were even remotely near my age, and I had no interest in his men whatsoever. But then Timothy saved my life.

I'd hate to see anything happen to him. He was someone I could relate to, and he had a way of making me happy. Although I hated to admit it, I was falling for him.

"Don't." I held up a hand. "You should leave here and go where they can't find you. Somewhere safe. Something is going on within the family, and I don't want you to get hurt." I drew in a deep breath. I'd stay, for now. "You're one of a kind. I mean that. You have a sweet heart, but it's going to end up causing you a lot of pain."

A smirk spread across his lips, and he glanced around the room. "Somehow, I doubt Little Boy came here because I'm a big softie inside. You know, under that B-class gangster vibe he gives out, there is a certain charm. I'm just glad I've avoided the full effects of his allure," he said in a serious tone before breaking out into laughter.

"Really? Is everything a joke to you?" I rolled my eyes. My mind played through Timothy and Little Boy trying to maintain an adult conversation before the two of them snuggled up on the couch. Absolutely ridiculous. I was tired, upset, and hurt. However, I couldn't hold in my laugh. The idiotic humor whisked away some of the tension between us.

"Not everything's a joke," he said, leaning in close. "What we have isn't a joke." His lips brushed against mine. "Thank you for meeting me tonight, for being with me here."

He tried to lean away, but I didn't want to let go. "You aren't getting away now." I slipped my tongue over the seam of his lips. For a moment, I wasn't sure if he'd allow me in, but he deepened the kiss, exploring my mouth.

*This is pure heaven.* All the worries of the day melted away. The comfort of his warmth, scent, and taste vanquished my darker thoughts and filled me with a giddy joy. As we pressed our bodies close to one another, I felt his firm shaft against my stomach. The soft, demanding ache to feel him became an imperative.

His hands dipped beneath my blouse, and he lifted it off. My body yearned to press skin against skin with him while I enjoyed the feeling of his warm, steady hands. His gaze slid over my body, taking in my curves. But I needed more. I pulled off his shirt, nibbling along his skin as I lifted the hem higher and higher. From his breathing, I could tell he was enjoying the moment.

"May I?" he asked when his shirt was out of the way.

I nodded and turned to let him unclasp my bra. The delicate, lace straps slipped down my arms and to the floor with our shirts, then the gentle touch of his hands circled around me, cupping my breasts. I moaned as he pressed kisses down my neck and across my shoulder. His fingers slid down my abdomen and dipped below the hem of my pants as far as the tight denim would let them. Biting my lip, I popped the button, urging him to go deeper.

And I certainly wanted him to go deep.

I tugged his hand away and turned in his arms.

We went to the bedroom, stripping off the remainder of our clothes on the way.

Timothy spread me out on the center of his bed, and my gaze drank in his body, unable to get enough. His muscles flexed and rippled as he crawled up the bed toward me. Our lips met again, and so did our bodies. Passion sparked between us hot like fire. We explored each other thoroughly, memorizing one another in fear that this could be our last time together. Time flew by as pleasure swept through us again and again.

But I wasn't afraid of what the future might hold or what my father would think about us. Timothy had survived under my father's thumb before I'd known him. Maybe we could make this relationship work. Besides, I knew I wouldn't be able to live with only one amazing night between us. Many more were needed.

# 7

## TIMOTHY

**B**eing with Letizia was like finding the missing piece of my life. The one thing that could bring me back from the brink and save me. Or, if her father found out about us, it could be my death.

Regardless, things were different now.

She was the first person I'd let get close to me in a long time, and now I wondered if maybe that was because I hadn't found the right one before. *Enough of that now. I've got a lot of work to do.*

I sat in front of my computer. The aging device wasn't too powerful anymore, but it was good enough to do internet searches and other online tasks. I began with cross-referencing the artifact and its history as far as the museum was able to provide, then traced its connection to the past.

Before making its way to London, the amulet had been part of the private collection of some big shot American movie director in the seventies. The man had filmed all over the world and had a tendency to buy souvenirs and oddities at each site he worked at. However, that information helped little with finding in-depth details on where the item had originated. Hell, he could've acquired it from the black market or some other private auction.

I ran my hands through my hair and turned to the second most reliable source, the item itself. Its metal composition and the scrollwork decoration would limit the source of origin.

The mix of metals with its various impurities would tell much about the way it was crafted—and guide me toward its origin. Again, the museum's website provided general composition facts, but no additional details on the item. While the antimony and tin amounts in the bronze mixture did point to Southern Italy, this was a dead end.

No metallic composition, no details on the text, and no easily traced history. *Damn.*

Pushing aside a stack of papers on my desk, I decided to start again with a clean sheet. I scribbled down my findings and moved on to other entries that I knew related to the necklace. For over an hour, I retraced everything I'd done and began comparing my notes with how the item came into my possession.

Strangely enough, no details existed on how or when the amulet had been brought into the museum. Each item typically mentioned that it had been acquired by the museum at an auction with a specific date, or had been donated to them as a part of someone's will. Instead, the artifact had seemingly been a part of a collection that trav-eled around. No mention of it existed until two weeks before it had arrived here, when it was suddenly included in the list upon visiting New Jersey before crossing the Atlantic.

Could explain why the police weren't looking for it. It didn't show up in catalogues before this one. There was no mention of when it had been added to the museum, no mention of who it had belonged to. Even anonymous donations were mentioned. The artifact just didn't exist on paper. News channels, the police, or anyone else had no clue it was missing. Perhaps someone from the staff might have an idea how an item they didn't have had appeared in their hallways.

Shite. I needed to go back to the museum.

One way or another, they'd have details of where it had come from. The staff normally kept immaculate records. Work receipts, placement orders, or written notes of which item would be placed where. Someone from the museum had to know it was missing.

Without a vehicle, it would be difficult to get there, and I didn't want to take public transport. If anything went wrong, I'd be trapped. A nagging thought reminded me of what took place last time. I shivered. Hopefully this time I wouldn't have to fight.

I headed to the bike locker. It'd been a while since I'd last used the bike, but I kept it in good shape. An innocent-looking man riding his bicycle through the city. Perfect. This might let me be more discreet. After all, who watched out for someone on a bike when they were looking for a thief?

I brought out the bike and hopped on. The first two miles were more painful than I remembered, but my usual rhythm soon returned to me. Feeling the wind on my face was exhilarating, and I found myself enjoying the freedom of it all. Thanks to the late evening, only two other people walked along the path to the museum. I stopped the bicycle near the edge of the museum's parking lot.

The wet grass beneath my shoes felt slippery. To my surprise, little evidence existed of the massive tree that had attacked me before. Whomever tended to the grounds was truly a master of their craft. Here and there, lighter green colored the grass betraying where the tree's roots had broken through the ground, but beyond that, the encounter seemed like nothing more than a bad dream. I stared into the mist for a few moments to make sure nothing else hid there. After two minutes, I made my way to the front door.

While it was late in the evening, the museum currently had extended hours. Maybe the press from the burglary had brought in fresh crowds. Besides, I was here only to ask questions about an item I'd seen during my previous visit. There was no reason for the staff to keep me from asking about the artifact's origins. I was merely a member of the public who wanted more details. With a pleasant smile on my face, I drew in a deep breath and walked in.

The museum looked different under the yellowish artificial light. During my previous visit, the place had been silent, but now the distant murmur of a crowd following a tour guide brought the hall to life. Occasional oohing and aahing about paintings and statues they passed made them easy to keep track of.

With a shrug, I walked up to the counter. "Can I talk to the museum's curator or someone like that?"

The receptionist glanced up from her magazine and frowned at me. "What?" She shook her head. "He's not in, but there's someone else you can speak to. Hold, please." After a quick call, she returned to reading her magazine. "Please take a seat. Someone will be with you shortly."

I didn't have to wait long.

A man in his early sixties soon made his way toward me. "I'm Benjamin Marley. How may I assist you?" he asked with sharpness in his tone. Obviously, my presence annoyed him.

"Thank you for meeting me, Mr. Marley. I was hoping

you could tell me something about an amulet I saw here the other day. I can't find it on display anywhere," I said.

The color drained from his face. Ah, I had a lead. "I know nothing of the sort. A heist happened here a few days ago, but I can guarantee, we had absolutely no amulets here. I'm more than happy to discuss the item if you would kindly describe it for me." The longer he talked, the shakier his voice became. My instincts went on high alert. He was hiding something and doing a poor job of it.

"Are you sure?" I pulled out a photo of the item. "I'm pretty sure this looks like your hallway there, past the Egyptian section." I pointed toward the two Ramesses II statues leading toward the exhibition.

Sweat trickled down his temple. "Come back to my office. Perhaps I can have a better look at that photo."

Without a word, we made our way past the heavy wooden doors separating the lobby from the staff area. My previous stroll in the building hadn't ventured here, but my mental map told me we were heading to a small, closed-off section. Soon enough, we took an elevator up to a floor that overlooked the exhibitions below.

"I have to say, I was hoping it'd take you longer to get here," Marley said cautiously. "It isn't often we lose an item that isn't particularly well documented." He opened the door to his office.

"There are ways. Why would anyone break into a museum and not steal anything, unless what they stole isn't even listed? Such things are self-evident if you pay attention." I waited for him to be seated. This verbal dance we played raked at my nerves. I carefully moved my left hand against the small throwing knife's hilt on my side as the older man sat behind his wide desk. I didn't like when people's hands were in places I couldn't see them.

"Really. We should have gotten some documentation from your masters to work this through. I told them it was too obvious to add yet another item to the hallway. But it matters little. Now the amulet is unprotected. Whoever stole it will soon act as a new vessel, and we will retrieve it as usual." He waved his hand dismissively.

What the hell? Again, I'd stumbled into something I shouldn't have known about.

*Keep a poker face, nod, and act the part.*

He wouldn't be pleased to know I had nothing to do with any of this. So I needed to convince him I did. I kept my gaze locked on his, hoping he bought whatever I was trying to sell.

"We are getting off subject, Mr. Marley. Someone has the artifact. If they know about it, they are surely searching for the other one, too." I lowered my voice as my gaze skimmed the office. "It would be a shame if my friends weren't able to retrieve the second piece first. It might be the end of you." That wasn't an exaggeration either. Little Boy would eat this guy for dinner. "I've seen what they do to those who fail. Trust me. There is pain far worse than death."

More sweat dripped down Marley's brow, and his hands trembled on his desk. Pushing him further—with no real knowledge of what this conversation truly meant—was dangerous, but my life would be over if I didn't get that second piece.

A vein pulsed visibly on the side of Marley's head as he contemplated his options. "They never mentioned the second piece, and it was never placed in the exhibition," he said. "Please, believe me."

This was a waste of time. If he didn't know anything about it, I was better off searching the internet again. I rose to leave, but he jumped to his feet, too.

"Wait! I know where it is. I never meant for any of this to happen, please. Don't send me back there. I'll do anything." Tears welled up in his eyes. Whatever they'd done to him in the past must have been quite traumatic. I hated the idea of poking at the man's old wounds, but in this case, I had little choice.

"Tell me. My time and yours is running out." I pointed at the square clock on his wall.

"Very well." Marley slumped his shoulders, looking utterly defeated. "Follow me."

We made our way to the elevator and descended to the lowest basement floor. The lights were dimmer and colder in color. The air felt dry and heavy with age, as if this place was significantly older than its surroundings.

Who was involved in this scheme Marley mentioned? I had no idea what I'd gotten wrapped up with, but it made me much less confident about this job. Heavy barred doors opened smoothly with the iron keys Marley fished out of his pants pocket. "It's in here." He waved me through the doors.

I shook my head and smirked. "I don't think so, Marley. I've played this game long enough. Walk ahead of me. I'm not falling for any traps."

Marley's face went pale as he stared past me.

From the corner of my eye, I saw a shadowy figure. It had been here during my last visit to the museum, too. Oh no. "Marley. Something is here. Maybe a shade. If you want to keep breathing, take me to the second piece. Hopefully, it'll be enough to keep us safe," I said, trying not to lose the thing from my peripheral vision.

"Then it's too late for one of us. And that won't be me." He scrambled to get past me and toward the elevator.

A quick jab to his chin with my elbow knocked him out cold. Oops. I hadn't meant to do that. Nearby, a bulb gave out, then another. Something paced at the edge of the cool light. Each time another bulb failed, a sensation of rushed movement pushed toward me, stopping barely at the light's edge. If I didn't do something quickly, I'd run out of light.

The flash of the next bulb breaking made me lose sight of the shade. *Bloody hell.* I grabbed Marley's keys and ventured down the now dark hallway. The less time I spent here, the better. A large storage area came into view up ahead. Crates lined the walls in various configurations. Heavy-duty metallic shelving supported some of the rows of boxes, while others were neatly stacked. Overhead lights did little to pierce the room's gloomy atmosphere. It was as if a blanket of smoke muted the light.

A clipboard hung from a nail at the entrance. It had a general plan for where items in the room were stored, along with a handwritten note saying the inventory was incomplete. Some sections needed to be inspected and moved. The logistical work was a nightmare, and the need for a good paper trail for each item became perfectly apparent.

Mentally crossing off sections where I didn't think Marley would've hidden the item, I focused on the Medieval, Renaissance, and Classical sections. Shelves upon shelves of items lined this section of the basement. The task would take a while, and not knowing where the eerie shadow was made my work all the more dangerous.

The heavy weight of the keys drew my attention. I'd walked through an old gate to get here, but there were other keys on the chain that didn't seem to belong. The smaller set, I dismissed as office keys used upstairs. No one with any awareness of how easy it was to pick certain locks would store anything of value behind them.

The rarer, semicircular key stood out. It was uncommon to see an Abloy key, which was resistant to bumping and general lock-picking tools. Looking around the room, I decided to focus on metallic containers. This might be slightly easier than I'd thought. No need to dig through all the crates, if I was lucky.

The first two containers in the Classical section were a bust. Keeping an eye on the containers and trying to watch for the shade was making the process slower than it should have been. Hidden behind a massive wooden box, I spotted the top of a small shipping container placed against the outer wall and a support beam. There was barely enough room to squeeze in between the two, which made me naturally curious. All other crates and boxes were easily accessible, so there was no reason to have a box somewhere so hard to reach.

Squeezing past the wooden box in front, I found an opening barely large enough for me to crack the door open. It was a little large for the amulet, but my suspicious mind thought it showed promise.

I looked around it first. There was a lock on the door, but something about this felt too convenient. The shade hadn't made an appearance, and I wondered if I was wasting my time here. With one of my longer-toothed lock picks, I gently probed along the side I couldn't see. Unable to feel anything—like alarm wires or other flaws in the metal—that would betray if it had been messed with, I focused on the lock itself.

The heavy padlock showed small signs of abuse, as if someone had tried to break in. Warily, I opened the lock and cracked the door. The shift of movement was the only warning I got. Even as I jumped away from the tight corner, a large claw swiped at me. The wound on my arm wasn't noticeable until I squeezed my way through the tight space between the boxes. Behind me, the loud sound of metal groaning and a door being forced open assaulted my ears.

The long-clawed creature was right behind me. Adrenaline surged through my veins, and I pulled myself onto the closest shelf and upward toward the top. Below me, the shelf wobbled as I felt more than heard wood breaking under the assault of the beast's sharp claws. It was a feline. That much I was certain about. It was quiet and quick, but the most troublesome aspect was I hadn't heard it breathe as it lunged for me. My mind worked through the details as I came to a stop on the top shelf. To my left, I found a box of Roman pottery. On the other side were remains of Greek theatrical masks. Nothing useful.

Where was the beast now? The shelf had stopped shaking, which made me nervous. In the center of the room, I saw the sleek, bronzed form of a tiger silently stalking back and forth. It craned its majestic head upward, metal flowing easily beneath its chin as if following the outlines of muscles.

I blinked, unable to believe my eyes. But it wasn't a trick.

The beast didn't breathe. No movement on its sides indicated the thing wasn't alive. When its paws moved, the tiniest metallic tick sounded as it connected with the concrete below. Its claws carried small strips of leather from my jacket. The thing was living metal, and I had no blowtorch at my disposal, let alone anything that could even put a dent in it. All I could do was sit and wait for its next move.

The tiger looked around the room before leaping to the edge of a low shelf, only to break through the wood and crash through somewhere underneath. It still carried the mass of an impressive bronze statue. At least it was heavy enough not to follow me up here easily. Still, if it had much intelligence, it'd tear the shelving apart and simply drop me to its level. From this height, I'd break something and be left vulnerable for the beast.

It tried again.

The silent malevolence of its movements, the tilt of its form, and the low, crouching approach betrayed its intent to kill. Once again, its weight was against it.

For a split second, I saw an overlap of the shade on the metallic beast. They both walked around, as if considering their options, then headed out to the hallway toward the elevators. Perhaps that shadowy being inhabited things or gave them an awareness to hunt? Both ideas were equally disturbing, but at least the beast was gone for now. Not knowing if it hunted by scent, sight, or sound, I didn't want to risk it tracking me as soon as I reached the ground.

I pulled a straw dummy from a crate, placed it on the ledge, and wrapped my torn jacket around it. If the beast returned, it might be distracted by the dummy instead of prowling for the real me. Trusting my padded shoes to soften the sounds, I made my way down the shelves onto the tiger's container. The sides were torn and bent where it'd forced its way out, and the lock was broken. Thankfully, the keys still sat on the concrete. I held them in my hand as quietly as possible and took another peek at what the container held.

Stone and metallic animals, one after another, stared at me lifelessly. Sweat rolled down my spine as I saw a small box on the floor of the container. It was a trap, but I'd already sprung it, right? If the tiger had been more patient, I'd be a dead man. What else could possibly go wrong? I reached for the box, even as I stared at the half a dozen statues that inhabited the container. The moment my hand brushed the outer edge of the box, I pulled it to me. Had something moved? Thoughts of all the animals coming to life in an instant made me panic. Not caring about the racket I was making, I ran full speed into the open and climbed onto the shelf again.

The only sound I could hear was the frantic beating of my heart. I pulled myself upward, thinking there had to be another beast behind me. As I made my way to the top once more, it became evident that nothing was following me, but the feeling of unease didn't go away. Maybe animating the beast took more energy out of the shade? I was relieved it hadn't chosen to animate everything distantly alive in the room to chase me.

But where the hell was the metal tiger? It was still loose.

I needed somewhere to hide here, but eventually, I had to get down. The only thing it had to do was sit in front of the elevators and wait. I hadn't seen stairs or an emergency exit on my way over, so I might be meeting the beast again eventually.

Sudden pained screams echoed through the hallway. *Oh, god...Marley.* The faint sound of ripping sickened me to my stomach. I'd never intended for the man to die. The screams went on for too long, as if the beast was toying with him. What had I done? Marley's screams finally ended, bringing a fresh, bone-chilling silence to the large room.

Forcing myself to remain calm, I pulled the jacket from the dummy and slid into it. Better it clawing my jacket than my flesh. Unfortunately, I needed to use this time while the beast was preoccupied. My mind raced to come up with ideas, until a thought finally hit me.

Looking around the basement, I searched for air ducts. On the other side of the room was a good-sized vent. Beneath it, a small maintenance platform was bolted to the wall. The vent most likely tried to guarantee the relative dryness of the storage area.

Luck was on my side after all. I headed for the vent, jumping from one set of shelves to another before I came to a sudden stop. From below me, I saw the glint of metal, prowling back and forth as if waiting for me to mess up.

The shelving stopped between the platform and me. Instead, boxes were stacked one on top of the other. The beast glared up me and began tearing apart the lowest boxes. The first two swipes were so fast I barely had time to register them. Had I been on top of the stack, I would've died. It tore apart my chance to escape, one box at a time.

It knew where I was, it knew where I was heading, and it placed itself in the gap it created. I'd seen cats jump. If this thing was capable of pouncing like its live counterpart, I had no chance.

Did I want to risk my life for this stupid amulet? No, but I was already screwed. If I didn't figure out a way out of here, I wouldn't live to see another sunrise.

I shuffled around to see if there was anything heavy enough to distract the beast with. It took me a moment to spot a long-forgotten pole. This might work once and only once. It'd been a while since I'd pole vaulted in high school, but my life depended on me not screwing up.

I held the ancient pole. The metal felt like it had lost some of its strength with age, but it only needed to get me across safely. It merely needed to hold together. Besides, I wasn't here to win any medals.

Taking a running sprint across the unstable shelf, I threw myself over the ledge and pushed the pole downward. It connected with the floor and carried my weight, then a snap jarred me as it crumbled from underneath, and gravity began to take hold. My momentum just barely carried me to the platform near the vent. *Ha!* The beast had been too slow. A roar from the creature startled me as the shade slowly blinked out of view. It had been beat. Who knew where it would go now? I had no intention of finding out.

Breathing a sigh of relief, I glanced down to find the motionless statue still staring at me with cold, lifeless eyes. Both halves of the pole lay at its feet. The victory was mine, and I cherished it. Now I needed to get out of here.

# 8

# TIMOTHY

The vents were a tight squeeze, but I made it through. Luckily, I'd taken a quick look at the museum's blueprints for my previous job, just on the off-chance I needed to use them.

When I made it to the yard, I brushed at my dust-covered clothes. My heart raced in my chest, but I made it out alive. The living metal tiger hadn't killed me, even though it tried its best, but this was far from over. Whatever was happening went way over my head.

Could it be the family was being set up for something much worse?

The job had been given to me through the normal channels, but after my discussion with Marley—poor bastard—I couldn't shake the feeling that much more was going on than it seemed. The way I'd been able to put pressure on the man, and how he'd cracked were obvious signs I was out of my league. Sure, I knew how to shake someone down to make them cough up money owed to the casino, but this was different.

A sense of dread washed over me.

All I knew was I needed to get out of here and pronto, so the shadow figure or whatever was in the basement couldn't follow me. I wanted to live a normal life and be rid of this shady side. The small, metal box in my pocket poked me again. Ouch.

Shrugging off my thoughts, I headed for my bike. I couldn't walk too fast or too slow. If I portrayed I was bored, having been around here a hundred times, and most importantly belonged here, I could get around without drawing much attention. With the recent news about the heist fresh in the public's thoughts, I suspected everyone was keeping an eye out for anything unusual.

Once I got to my bike, I saw a man approaching me. His clothing stuck out like a sore thumb. The well-pressed, deep blue jacket and his aristocratic stride spoke of someone with affluence and power. I'd met his kind in my job before, and they usually had volatile tempers.

"Sir. May I speak with you a moment?" His crisp accent was sophisticated but carried with it an authority. If I'd drawn the attention of the NCA, my days were numbered.

"Of course. How can I help you?" My answer sounded intrigued, even to my own ears.

"Do you have any thoughts on the current museum exhibits? Maybe you wouldn't, though. Terribly sorry to bother you with such a question, but it strikes me as odd to see a man walking around here covered in filth. You couldn't possibly have been inspecting the area, now could you?" His lips curved into a predatory smile—ravenous and void of warmth. The man knew much more than what he let on.

"I have gone through the museum's exhibits. I particularly enjoyed seeing the Shabti dolls and learning about their importance to ancient Egyptian afterlife." Dealing with Alonzo and his goons had helped perfect my poker face, so I kept my tone and expression pleasant.

Even though his remarks about inspecting the area struck close, it seemed he wasn't quite aware of what had taken place. Or maybe he was trying to withhold that information? Seemed unlikely, though.

"Good day to you, sir," I said and turned back to my bicycle.

"I must insist you stay a bit longer. All will be revealed soon enough, Timothy. After all, your friends took their time in dealing with your car, and it's not difficult to locate car owners through their license plates. Besides, yours was tangled up in a tree. Would you kindly provide an explanation for that?" The smile on his face never wavered. He knew my name—and likely much more.

It felt my whole world was caving in on me. What the hell was I going to do? I couldn't tell the truth.

"I'm puzzled by that, too. I brought my car here after drinking a few too many beers. You know how expensive London parking is. Figured with the fog it wouldn't be safe to drive home. I walked over to that path there to relieve myself when suddenly...*woosh!* My car was on fire. Damnable fog made my walk home abysmal. I could barely see a foot in front of me. What am I going to tell my insurance? It's better to admit I don't have a clue what happened instead of getting locked up for a psych eval somewhere." I hoped he wouldn't press me too much. "So, what should I call you, sir?"

"I'm not sure we're quite ready for that now, Timothy. But I will keep an eye on you. I have a feeling we'll meet again soon." As he turned to leave, I caught a glimpse under his jacket. Two pistols hung on either side, camouflaged by the jacket's padding. It was no mistake. He'd let me see them.

A chill seeped into my bones. Whoever he worked for seemed to have no qualms with violence. In that instant, I knew he wasn't with the NCA but someone far more dangerous.

# 9

# LETIZIA

Rain dripped almost lazily against the windowpane. Once again, fog clung to the afternoon air. I sat in the window seat in my bedroom and hugged a pillow to my chest. Thoughts of Timothy and the love we'd made last night danced through my head. However, they also worried me. I didn't want anything to happen to him. My attraction to him had grown with the intimacy.

The grandfather clock chimed.

The house was particularly active, even though everyone seemed exhausted. My father looked like he hadn't received a good night's sleep in days, and most of the staff didn't look any better themselves.

"Letizia, come." My father's quick knock on the door drew my attention. "I want you to sit in on the family meeting with your cousin, Roberto."

"I'll be right there, Papa."

He expected me to go over some details with Roberto about his restaurant and look at his plans for the next quarter. The meeting itself was pretty dull. My cousin didn't have much drive or efficiency. It was pretty obvious the restaurant wasn't his main source of income. There was no way he'd drive an Aston Martin with his business looking like this. I'd expected better, but Roberto seemed pretty pleased with himself.

With the grey weather, I barely managed to stay awake, and my father proved remarkably quiet as well.

Tony, one of my cousin's business partners, cleared his throat. The talking among everyone quieted down. "Don Prosdocimi, I promise we'll give you better results next time. I'll take it upon myself to make sure you're pleased."

My cousin and his other partners lifted their voices in agreement at once, as if just now noticing my father's silence and taking it for displeasure. Idiots.

Something was bothering him, but I doubted it was Roberto's restaurant. I wanted to shake away the doubt that he'd somehow learned of my interest in Timothy, but the nagging thought wouldn't leave me.

Later when we had afternoon tea, he barely lifted his head from the notes and numbers I'd written during the meeting. He couldn't be that interested in them, but his eyes were in constant motion.

"Papa? Is something wrong?" He didn't react to my voice, as if I hadn't said a word. Was he upset with me and trying not to show it?

I nibbled on the edge of a scone, letting its flavor mix with the Earl Grey tea. While I wanted to get him out of his headspace and to share his thoughts, I knew that came with the risk of him blowing up. By the time I finished my second cup of tea, I'd had enough. He could find me when he was ready to talk.

From the drawing room where we'd had tea, I headed to the library. To my surprise, no signs of the shooting that had taken place here were visible, but my mind still froze in fear for a brief moment as I opened the heavy doors. Any danger that existed here was gone. Sooner than later, I'd need to get over that incident.

I let the pictures and paintings of my ancestors lining the walls lure me in. The images of my family comforted me as I made my way to the shelves.

As I roamed around the stacks to find a book to pass my time with, I noticed the arrangement had changed. I'd spent enough time in the library that the visual layout of the books had become embedded in my mind. Tracing a finger over the spines, I spotted the out-of-place book and pulled it aside.

*What's this?* I turned it over in my hands.

Inside, my father's handwriting chronicled our artifacts, detailing their origins. The family history recorded in this book was precious and valuable. Why on earth would he have left it here?

I shook my head.

I'd seen the journal many times, of course. Detailed descriptions of family armor, a sword, or a painting depicting a nobleman of the family lined its pages. Markings on the pages' edges indicated where the item was stored at, if it had been acquired, and so on.

I started to close the book, but the pages flipped to a section deeper inside. My gaze caught a sketch of the amulet he'd recently acquired. The markings were slightly confusing. It looked like it was two pieces that had once been separate necklaces. A smith in Florence had crafted a hidden mechanism that allowed the two pieces to overlap and lock together.

What really caught my eye were the red markings along the paragraph. My father used red pen only when he wanted to be sure whoever read the journal wouldn't miss his words. The necklace contained lead, so prolonged exposure would be damaging to whoever handled it. Next, it detailed how our ancestors had managed to obtain the artifact, only to be driven insane and lose it again. *That's curious...and unsettling.*

Eventually one of my great aunts, who didn't have any children, came across it and held onto it despite the family's wishes. Over the years, she became an alcoholic and increasingly withdrew herself from society, until finally my great grandfather intervened. They drove her from her home and sent her away to the United States.

It had broken her heart. She became bitter and lonely, caring only for herself. Too proud to work, she relied on the family's name to abuse the local Italian immigrants. When they eventually refused to support her, she sold the necklace to finance her spiraling alcoholism. She passed away shortly after, and all traces of the item went cold.

The story itself had corrections throughout, but what worried me were the more recent details that had changed. My father had altered her circumstances. In an older version, she'd acquired the artifact first, then became an alcoholic. With his latest correction, she'd been an alcoholic before the necklace was gifted to her. Where had he found this new information? Besides, the extent of the edits he'd made weren't typical of him.

Once he wrote something on the page, he needed infallible evidence to make him redo a section. However, he'd hastily rewritten almost half of the page here. It didn't make sense. I closed the book and held it against my chest. I'd return the journal to his study.

Papa was no longer focused on business, nor did he seem to be as aware of his surroundings as before. It worried me. Was he suffering from some sort of medical ailment?

Perhaps if nothing else worked, I'd call in a favor with other members of the family so they could talk with him. Hopefully, he would listen to them. We all needed him to be focused, and whatever was troubling him as of late needed to be solved.

I knocked on the door to his study and was greeted with a surprisingly cheerful reply.

"Come in." His pleasant tone helped to settle my nerves a little.

"I'm sorry to bother you, Papa, but you left this in the library," I said, seeing that I'd interrupted him from talking with one of our bodyguards. What was going on?

His gaze darted to the leather cover and back to me before he waved his hand at the bodyguard. "Go. We'll finish this later. Just make sure we have enough reinforcements available if we need them." With the bodyguard dismissed, he returned his full attention to me. He gestured me to come closer. "I don't recall misplacing the journal, but I'm glad you found it. It's most valuable to this family."

I stepped up to his desk and set the book down before him. "It is. I look forward to taking over work on it when my time comes. Family means a lot to me." Hopefully, he caught my full meaning, but his gaze remained on the book instead of meeting mine.

When he finally looked up, I nearly stepped back. Something wasn't right with his eyes. They kept moving, as if he were having trouble with his sight. "Is it just me, or is it slightly dark in here?" The question just confirmed my concerns. After a few moments, he shook his head and lifted his gaze to mine once more. This time, his eyes were clear and focused.

"I'm sorry. It seems all this worrying about the new expansion has me more on edge than I should be. Thank you for bringing up the diary. That was kind of you, darling. Now I need to ask you to run along. I have to deal with some of the more dissatisfactory matters of business," he said. The tone he used was a strange one, as if I was a kid again. I knew about the other side of the business. But I'd give him the space he needed.

"Just remember to take breaks and don't work too hard, Papa." I turned to leave.

Our family, like every business out there, had to see their leader was in charge. Unless Papa snapped out of his funk, our business partners might begin to distance themselves. Then someone else might rise up and make our lives so much worse, if we were allowed to keep them at all.

I closed the door to his study on my way out. Mario, one of the family's accountants, came my way. If my father didn't handle the day-to-day operations, I'd have to step up. Did I want to run the family business? Was I ready for that kind of responsibility?

Not a chance, but it needed to be done.

So much needed to be done in order to guarantee those we employed were backed by the family. Stability, reliability, and a recommendation were incredibly important. Money bought many things, but an untarnished name wasn't one of them.

"If I could have a moment of your time, Miss Letizia," Mario said. "This shouldn't take too long, and I know your father is..." He paused as if trying to find the right words. "Let's say a busy man these days."

That was a polite way of putting it.

"Sure, I have time." Not that I wanted to deal with this right now. I'd much rather head back to my bedroom and think about when I'd see Timothy again, but this was probably for the best.

We sat at the conference table in the library where we went over the family's accounts, two salary changes, and the continued business deal with Roberto. I noticed my father had increased our internal security and bodyguard count in the past few days. How odd. What was he so afraid of?

The move didn't really impact our running budget, but the additional guards might draw attention from the other families and the police. Our family was being watched by various agencies, so news like this would spread rapidly. Word needed to hit the streets to calm things down. But could I approach my father about this, or should I handle it on my own?

Maybe it could be spun. The London bombing had many on edge recently. We were simply trying to protect our own. A sense of relief spread through me. It was an easy lie to sell. My father had always been a reasonable man. He was currently helping the neglected asylum, after all. He'd want to ensure our friends and customers were well protected. We were here for the community as well as our business.

My head hurt as we finished going over the books.

Mario kept other folders out of reach, and I hoped there weren't more concerns hidden within them. They likely contained information from the less pleasant side of my father's business. Money laundering, protection money, and illegal gambling profits were just a few of those grey areas. Still, from what I'd seen, I couldn't help but be concerned.

The other part of me was just fine with closing my eyes, putting my fingers in my ears, and not touching that. If I went my whole life uninvolved with the illegal side, I'd be happy.

Soon enough, Mario began putting away the folders once more. "That's all for now. Ciao, Miss Letizia."

"Thank you for keeping me informed." I leaned back in my chair and smiled at him as he left. But on the inside, I wished there was something I could do to stop whatever was going on with my father. We were family, and family looked out for one another.

## 10

## LETIZIA

The house had fallen quiet once more. My father had gathered those who regularly worked with him in his study to review how things were going. Strictly off-limits to me, of course, but that didn't stop me from finding out what was going on. The house's heating system relied on an old-style radiator that pumped hot water. The pipes carried more than warmth.

I sat close to one, hearing the echo of voices.

At one time, I considered sharing this secret with my father in hopes that he'd prevent just anyone from listening in to secret information, but now I was glad I hadn't. While I wasn't invited into the room, I'd seen Timothy being brought into the house. His jacket was in tatters and the expression on his face was grim. I hoped he had good news and we'd have a chance to sneak away again soon. I missed the feeling of his warm body against mine.

As I focused on the discussion in the room, I knew Timothy wasn't in there. One of the men who dealt with the police noted how their activities near the docks hadn't gone unnoticed, and the usual tariffs had been doubled for their mistake. Every few months, the police would crack down a house belonging to us and drag one or two of our associates to the streets to show how active and successful they were at stopping crime. Behind the scenes, they'd take a 'donation,' and *poof*. The evidence vanished from the locker.

The rest of the discussion went along without interruption until my father was informed of Timothy's arrival. With all other business concluded, they agreed to bring him into the room. Heavy footsteps banged through the pipes, muffling all other sounds for the moment.

"How nice of you to join us. You have something to share, isn't that right?" My father's voice held a sting of impatience.

"Yes, but you need to be careful. Something isn't right with all of this." Timothy sounded concerned. "Who told you where the first piece was?"

"You don't get to ask questions. Your job is to do as you're told." There was a small pause. "Ah, you brought me the second piece, a piece that belongs to my family and mine alone. I will allow nothing to ruin this moment." My father's voice exuded stubborn authority. Was that a slur to his words, too? That was out of place for him. It'd been a long time since my father heavily turned to drink. After my mother died, actually. Was he drinking again? Ever since he'd gotten the first piece of that damn amulet, he'd been acting different.

The pipes beside me hissed as a few bubbles of air moved through them. When I could follow the conversation again, I heard Timothy explain how he'd been able to acquire the piece. A living metal tiger statue tried to attack him? If I hadn't seen his ripped-up jacket, I'd have thought he was absolutely mad.

Little Boy burst into a fit of laughter. "You think we really believe this fairytale shite of yours? Moving statues, ghosts, and all that other crap? You must think we look stupid here, don't you? Little thief, just wait until we no longer need—" He was abruptly cut off by the bang of a fist on the table.

"He completed the job," my father said. "He managed to find it when I had also asked you to look for it. I would be careful there, Little Boy. Mr. Sands, you've done me a favor. Now, please head downstairs and collect your payment. I have other business that requires my attention."

My heart raced, and I released a breath I didn't realize I'd been holding. Good, it was done. Maybe I could catch him on the way out.

As I climbed to my feet, a barely audible voice came through the pipes that chilled me to the core. "He's sleeping with her, you know," Little Boy said.

"Explain yourself! What are you talking about?"

"I believe Sands is sleeping with your daughter. Giulia from the restaurant told me she spotted Miss Letizia there with a young man. When I questioned her, the mystery man fit Sands's description. One of my men who's been watching his place saw her leaving his residence last night. I should've said something sooner, but—"

"No, I want to speak with this man of yours. I can't believe my daughter would do this." He let out an angry grunt. "Sands? No. He can hardly be considered a man. Nor does he know how to dress. I very much doubt he could charm anyone of our standing, let alone my daughter."

"Boss, please calm down. When I dropped by his place to give him the job, I saw her Givenchy purse on the kitchen counter."

"Leave me!" My father's voice carried through the pipes with enough force to make me flinch.

From the fading steps, I could tell Little Boy did as my father asked.

Afraid of what would happen next, I continued to listen in. My father paced back and forth in the room. Soft muttering slowly built up into a monologue that he only did when something had him badly worked up. That rarely happened, but he'd already been on edge.

Part of me hated Little Boy now. I had a feeling the only reason he dropped his bombshell was to get back at Timothy for my father sticking up for him. He likely had been trying to gather more evidence against him before making the case to my father.

Suddenly my father grew quiet, then sinister whispers began as if another person was in the room with him. I could make out a few words here and there, and what I heard made me fear for my father's sanity. He'd locked himself up alone a lot recently, and now he was talking with someone whose words I couldn't hear. The one-sided conversation continued, and I knew it wasn't a call. The study was built to prevent cell signals from working within the room.

"Should I connect the two amulets? I'm not sure if it's a good idea, my aunt." He seemed to be crying, or maybe he was snickering? It was hard to tell, but each time he paused, he made those strange sounds. "I have a plan. It justifies everything I've done so far. It will make you proud of me."

His tone suddenly changed. "No, Mr. Sands didn't intend to hurt me through my daughter. He's been a good man to me and mine. My daughter..." He paused to take a deep breath.

The pipes hissed again. However, for a moment, I thought I heard a female voice in the room, another presence simply too quiet to be heard. But that didn't make sense. My family didn't allow others in there. Aside from kitchen staff and a housekeeper, we didn't have many women in the house.

My father's crying grew into sobs. The pain in his voice made it clear something had broken in him, as if he'd lost someone dear to him.

Fear coiled in my gut.

"Yes, my aunt. They will suffer like I've suffered. If either one thinks my word means nothing, I will show them. Letizia will know my pain when I rip out Sands's heart myself!"

I cupped my hands over my mouth to hold in a gasp. Tears welled in my eyes. *Oh no! No, no, no...* I couldn't sit back and do nothing with this information. Timothy needed to know.

"There's another way, you say? I understand you want to deal with him personally, but are you certain you want me to connect the amulets already?" He hesitated a moment. "Fine. I will do this for you. Do as you wish."

An almost deranged laughter echoed from the pipes, and the atmosphere in the entire building changed, as if suddenly the world had been shaken like a snow globe.

Dizziness swayed me on my feet, but I had to find Timothy before it was too late.

## 11

# TIMOTHY

The meeting went pretty smoothly, even if Little Boy had been a dick, but this would be the last payment I needed in order to get even. After this, I could forget this half of my life and finally move on.

Being a prisoner to past mistakes was something I wanted for no one. As I reached the bottom of the stairs, I saw Letizia waiting there. Something was wrong. That much was clear from her reddened face and teary eyes. She motioned me without words to follow her to one of the rooms.

"Are you okay?" I wanted to wrap her in my arms and comfort her. "What's wrong?" I asked after she pulled me into the room.

"You need to leave. They know." Her voice cracked with emotion. "Little Boy knows I was at your place, and he told my father." I pulled her close to me, needing the comfort now. This was bad. Really bad. "Stop it. You have to leave. I'll try to call you," she said, pushing at my chest. But she wouldn't meet my eyes, as if there was more she refused to share with me.

"How did he know? We were careful."

"He saw my purse, and someone was watching your flat." She collapsed against my chest, as if the fight had been drained from her. "Please, you need to leave. I'm scared of what they'll do to you if you don't go soon. Please."

I wanted to stay. She meant more to me than I'd thought possible. But to never see her again? I'd rather have her than break free from my debt. She was the one. I knew it in my heart. From the moment I'd laid eyes on her, she'd been on my mind.

"I will see you again. This doesn't have to end between us." I pressed a kiss to her forehead, then left as tears caressed her cheeks.

Now I had to get out of here. There was little time to waste. Chances were high that they'd send someone to catch me, and I had no intention of being caught in the family's drama. To avoid suspicion, I would do as I was told. Go to one of Alonzo's assistants and get paid.

In the sitting room, Henry was seated in a comfortable armchair with a clipboard on his lap. He never said much. The exchange took less than a minute, and I folded the cashier's check into my jacket pocket and closed the zipper. I hadn't nearly died just to lose the check at the last moment.

As I neared the outer door, I spotted people right outside the entryway. Their shapes were easily visible from the frosted glass panel.

*Bloody hell. Think fast.*

Rather than use the front door, I headed for the staircase to my right. If I made it to the roof, I might be able to leave via a fire escape. Even as I took my first step on the stairs, I knew it had been a trap. The outer door opened, and someone came down from one of the higher floors. Taking a few steps back, I spotted the alcove under the stairs, ducked in the shadows, and remained utterly still.

The heavy steps from above came to eye level, then continued into the lobby. The back of the man's grey head revealed it had only been the butler. So, it hadn't been a trap after all. Maybe my paranoia was through the roof after Letizia's revelation. I let out a small sigh of relief. Taking a few cautious steps up the stairs, I heard arguing from the lobby, where Henry was answering a guard's demanding questions about where I'd disappeared to. The less they were aware of, the better. I quietly picked up my pace.

The second floor was expansive, mostly overlooking the lobby. It had various chairs and lounging space all around with ornate stained-glass windows decorating the walls. It was only a matter of time until someone saw me.

Enjoying the padding on my boots, I darted toward a hallway where the stairs further up would likely be. An alarmed yell from below told me one of the hired muscle knew where I was. Soon I heard footfalls from all sides, but I wasn't going to give up.

Running past a nearby bookcase, I was met with a massive fist to my side. The force of it spun me around, but I didn't stop. Letting the momentum carry me further, I leaned into it, allowing the padding of my jacket to take the brunt of the impact against the wall. But my legs slid out from under me, spilling me to my arse on the floor.

Little Boy came into view from an alcove beside the large bookcase with a smile playing on his lips. "The boss isn't quite done with you, slick. You need to spend a little time with the rest of the family, too. We want to know more about the man who has shown such interest in the sweet and inno-cent Letizia, don't we?" The grin on his face told me all I needed to know.

He kicked me on the side he'd punched me in before. A small, black box in his hand barely registered with the spark of electricity that flared off it.

Shite. "Taser. Do you really need something like that?" I laughed at him and tried to move, but pain made my movement agonizingly slow.

He jabbed the Taser against my chest.

My chest muscles spasmed like a bad cramp where he was pressing, then my entire body seized up, unable to move. Overwhelming pain filled my entire existence. When he finally pulled away, my body slid the rest of the way to the floor, and I stared up at the ceiling

"Well, it seems to do the trick. You aren't going anywhere. Right? Now, behave. If you do, I'll let you die with some honor before this is done." Something in his eyes told me he'd do no such thing. Still, I wasn't going to mouth off and be beaten senseless. I preferred to potentially be able to move if a window of opportunity revealed itself.

He took my lack of words for a yes and called for his little troop to pick me up. The first man flipped me over and tied my hands, then the second one hit me with his Taser just because he could.

As I was dragged over the floor, face down on the marble, they managed to break my nose and split my lip on a few steps before we finally came to a halt in a service elevator. We headed down. That was the only thing I could tell. The two of them kept flinging threats about what was going to happen, but I paid them no attention. Instead, all my focus went on getting my legs to function again.

The torture room, the execution room, the interrogation room—I didn't care where they dragged me to. It smelled like one or the other. The stench of urine, blood, and shite mixed with fear and terror. Add poor lighting to that, and I wondered what they had in store for me.

My captors wasted little time tying me to an old, wire-frame chair. The metal seat dug into my skin even through the thick clothes. I tested the balance on it and found the chair could easily be knocked to the side if necessary. Not only that, but it would allow me to possibly roll with the punches, transferring some of the impact to a rocking motion against the chair.

It didn't take long until the first few hits started landing against my stomach. Air rushed out of my lungs, but I didn't give them the satisfaction of groaning or wincing. It seemed to frustrate the two guards, and their punches came harder and faster. Each time they hit on the center or the left side, I was able to get the chair to move in time to transfer the impact, but my right side hit by the second Taser still refused to cooperate.

A sudden hush fell over the room as Alonzo Prosdocimi entered. His demeanor had changed. Where he'd been a passionate man when we'd met minutes ago, he seemed somehow defeated now. A sick, sweaty sheen clung to his skin, as if he had a fever. The pale tones in his complexion made it evident something was drastically different. Even the guards who had been pummeling me seemed a little taken aback.

"You'll be like the rest of the rats who thought they were good enough for my daughter, you know? But you're not the type to be fazed by your own death. Instead, I'll drag everyone you love down here and torture them in front of you. And before they die, wondering why they're here, I'll let them know you're responsible. Little Boy will find your brother first, then search for others you care about. When you've got nothing left, I'll give you a sense of freedom, a sense of meaning and peace, and then I'll take it away again. You'll know my pain, little thief," he said, his voice shaky and weak.

His shoulders hunched forward, and he looked like a broken man. Had my relationship with Letizia really impacted him this badly? But that didn't make sense. A sickly feeling rose in my stomach as I saw his lips move slightly, as if he was talking to something else in the room. In his closed fist, I saw the outer edges of the artifacts now joined together.

"What did you do?" I asked, looking him square in the eye.

He hesitated, as if a part of him wondered that too, but it was quickly replaced by another shiver. "What every man would do for his only daughter. You don't know what it's like to lose something so precious," he sneered and walked away.

Lose something? He still had his daughter. Unless...

I needed to get out of here, and fast, for both myself and Letizia.

More blows landed on my sides and my face, but they hurt less than the knowledge he might do something to his own daughter. The man I'd worked for had become a puppet to something terrible that was tied to the artifacts. I shouldn't have taken the job. My brother had been right. It would've been better to leave the necklace buried and forgotten.

## 12

## LETIZIA

Father was entirely absent during supper, focusing more on the newspaper than looking at me or paying attention to my questions. He looked terribly ill, too. And when he did look at me, his expression became severe and almost sinister. Part of me wanted to ask what he'd done with Timothy, but the other didn't even want to be in the same room as him.

The meal had been a light soup, which barely managed to satisfy me. Midway through the meal, I excused myself and headed to the kitchen. While I cut a slice of bread for myself, Little Boy marched in. His eyes darted to the knife and then back at me.

"Easy there, girl. We wouldn't want to do anything rash, isn't that right?" His voice was sickly sweet and all honey, a clear sign he'd let his violent side loose recently. Could that be related to the commotion I'd heard earlier? He almost danced in the kitchen behind me, making himself a sandwich loaded with meats and cheeses. "We're having a little party tonight. Feel free to join us, if you want. But first, I need to run a small errand," he said before disappearing again.

All the time he was there, I never let go of the knife. Something about him screamed at me not to trust him. I'd seen him become a maniac at the drop of a hat. Besides, he'd told my father about me and Timothy. Although he'd never shown me any interest, I knew that could change in a heartbeat, and I had no intention of turning up in an alley, carved up from thighs to ears.

Once his heavy footsteps faded, I headed to my room with the sandwich I had made for myself. My father would've said this wasn't ladylike, but I didn't care. The watery soup wasn't enough to keep my hunger away right now, and his presence made me uneasy. After all, while I loved my father, he'd also said he would rip Timothy's heart out to cause me pain.

I latched my bedroom door, not wanting to deal with anyone else tonight. The heavy bolts my family had insisted remain installed on the bedroom doors were one of the things I appreciated about the old house. They would do little to keep anyone away for an extended time, but with each room having firearms available at a moment's notice, it mattered little.

I walked to a small desk near the windows at one end of my room to set my plate down.

Timothy should've reached his home by now, and I wanted to see if he was okay. So what if we dated? It wasn't my father's concern. My life could pass me by before I'd find a man my father would approve of. He would never let me go. How many men had tried to pursue me only to end up disappearing? Each time I'd cried and ran to Papa for comfort, until I discovered what was really going on.

After eating my sandwich, I felt a little better, and my hunger had subsided.

If Timothy was still in the house, I should wait until later to look for him. The guards changed shifts at two o'clock, and usually took their time talking about sports and life. A big football game was on tonight, which would draw most of their attention anyway.

The door didn't budge as I tried to open it. Something was blocking me in, and it was solid. My heart raced in my chest. What was going on? My father had never done something like this before. I might've been a prisoner in the house, but I'd never been locked in my room. Dread coiled in my gut as my thoughts drifted to the heavy oak cabinet that usually sat a little ways down the hall. No way would I get out of here without help. Ramming my shoulder against the door would only hurt me and draw unwanted attention.

Maybe this could work to my advantage. My gaze darted to the other way out of the room, the wide windows overlooking the gardens.

I didn't have enough sheets to climb down, so I rejected that idea as soon as I saw the distance to the wet grass. Breathing in the fresh air, I concentrated on my next move and looked around for ledges. As a teen, I'd often wondered if I could escape through the window when my father was upset at me, but I never dared to do anything so dangerous. However, Timothy was worth the risk. The stone walls were too wet to be scalable, but the roofing outcrop intended to keep water from hitting the window was just above me.

The old wooden structure looked sturdy, but there weren't many places to grab on to. I turned my back to the windowsill and looked up, planning my move out of here. Four wooden crossbeams supported the platform. Two of them were along the roof, most likely starting from somewhere underneath the masonry. The other two took support from the wall itself. There wasn't much room, but maybe I could place my hands on both sides and inch my way over to another window or the roof itself.

Not wanting too many cuts, I wrapped my hands in two pillowcases from my closet. Pulling myself onto the ledge was harder than I'd anticipated, and I was glad I'd protected my hands in the soft satin. I shifted my weight a little, moving my left arm to support myself on the right beam. All the while, I prayed the added weight wouldn't bring the entire thing down.

Ten seconds passed, and a wide arc of light swung around me.

A guard patrolling the garden waved a flashlight around the rooftops. What did he hope to accomplish with it in the thick fog? It was beyond me, but he must've heard my movements. *Oh no.* The squawk of a radio and his voice came up from the fog.

"Can I get someone to the roof to verify everything is as it should be? I thought I saw something."

"I'll be right up, mate."

The exchange made my muscles tense. Now I'd have to wait for someone to get to the roof? I pulled myself back beneath the old wooden structure again and waited. My arms burned by the time the other guard reached the roof and looked around. These men my father employed took pride in their work as they inspected the roof. I was glad they were on our payroll, but couldn't they be a bit more relaxed today?

By the time I made it to the roof, my arms were painfully sore. *Timothy, I hope you're not here.* In a stroke of luck, the guards who checked out the roof had left the rooftop access door unlocked. The warm air behind the door and the darkened hallway was inviting after dangling off the side of the mansion. I nearly sighed with relief. But this was nowhere near where I needed to be. I'd stumbled upon the lowest floors of the house before. If Timothy was in the house, they were keeping him there.

The guards and other staff moved all on the lower floors. The closer I came to the kitchen, the more I had to hide in the nooks and crannies of the old house.

While the game had many of the guards somewhat distracted, it also made them more unpredictable. Where there were usually only a handful of guards in the house, today it was packed. Supporters of both sides made trips to the bathroom and the kitchen on a regular cadence. Little by little, I pushed into the kitchen. The warm wooden paneling of the kitchen changed to old, dry tile and brick as I descended into the basement. No moisture clung to the walls, but the earthen scent of the basement was still heavy in the air. My soles echoed against the old stone floor, so I removed them and continued barefoot.

My father had renovated part of the basement to include a small service lift and other conveniences, like soundproofing. After all, this place was important for his darker activities. The guests above never knew what went on beneath their feet.

Shoving those thoughts aside, I tiptoed through the hallway to the older section of the basement. I stopped in front of the doors leading to the renovated section and waited. Walls could easily be soundproofed, but doors were more difficult. The quiet sounds escaped from under the heavy rubber seals at the bottom of the door. Two guards talked about how incredible the game had been. My watch told me it was only five minutes until two. Waiting around was more tedious than I'd have thought. It wasn't the passing of time itself. It was being so close to the truth and having to wait.

I balled my hands into fists and imagined myself slamming them into the door over and over. The ding of the elevator nearly escaped my notice, but the sound was a welcome relief.

*The shift change.*

I cracked the door, then slowly walked in. A set of screens draped with plastic sheeting covered my entrance, but I was relying on the fact no one would expect me there. The door closed quietly behind me, and I made my way farther into the basement.

The two guards waited in front of the elevator for their replacements to arrive. Their eyes were focused on the doors, hands holding their automatic firearms. The men were definitely on edge tonight. Slowly, I continued my trek deeper into the basement. While they were so focused on what was in front of them, I made my way behind their backs. With each step I took, I feared they'd turn around, drawn by some noise or a shadow playing across the room.

A set of extended cells stood ahead of me. I wanted to barge into them and find out where Timothy was, but I knew better. Slow and steady would be the only way of getting him to safety. A black plastic sheet separated the entrance to a new section from the holding cells. Thankful for the sheeting, I went for the closest door. The other side bore an eerie silence. A quick peek into the room revealed a wire-framed chair and a bucket.

The next two rooms held nothing of importance either —one of them was stained heavily with dried blood, and the other was as pristine as if it had been painted yesterday. *The last door. It has to be the one.* Pressing my ear against the door, I heard the sound of flesh being hit and crude, snorting laughter. Without thinking, I picked up a pipe from the corner and quietly opened the door.

The laughter echoed off the walls as a young man landed blow after blow to Timothy's stomach. His attention to his gruesome work was singular, so he never saw the pipe swinging toward his head. The man fell to the ground.

I raised the now bloodied weapon again. My hands shook, and only when I heard my name whispered, did I realize Timothy was alive. Tears ran down my cheeks. The horror of what I'd done came over me. "I didn't mean to," I said, laying the pipe on the ground.

All that mattered now was holding Timothy close and getting us out of here. I knelt next to the man and slid the keys out of his pocket. I took deep, gasping breaths as I tried to tame my emotions and focus on the present. *Get Timothy out. Cry later.* Even so, I nearly broke into sobs as I helped him out of the chair. His body was bruised and so badly beaten. The muscles I'd snuggled against not too long ago were now angry shades of red and smeared with blood.

I massaged his weary limbs for a few minutes since his legs refused to hold him. We couldn't walk out of here. He was in no condition to run. His breath hissed through his clenched teeth with every unsteady step. It was a miracle we made any progress at all.

## 13

# TIMOTHY

With Letizia's help, I limped my way from the mansion's grounds, but we couldn't let our guard down now. My muscles ached as I tried to move my beaten body. Letizia's support was the only thing keeping me on my feet. Clenching my jaw, I pushed ahead into the thick patch of trees. There was no way out. We couldn't get away from them on foot, and sooner than later, someone would notice I was missing.

"Our chances are slim. Getting out of here before they realize I'm gone...? I don't think it's possible." I frowned down at her. "Please, go back to the mansion. Your chances might be better if they think you're innocent."

Her face scrunched into an angry glare. "What are you talking about? I didn't get you out of there so you could sit down and give up. I know this won't be easy. I...I killed one of the family to free you." Her voice trembled, and she gently caressed my cheek. "We're in this together now. Don't you know that? I care about you, and I won't see you hurt." She handed me my cell phone.

As much as I didn't want to agree, she was right. Besides,

it seemed like a matter of time before Alonzo snapped, and I knew he couldn't be trusted with his daughter's life. "I won't give up. I just don't want you to get hurt either. But you're right. They won't be happy with one of the men being killed."

I looked at my phone. It was better than nothing, but if I called anyone in the business, they'd betray our where-abouts to the men in the mansion. Our escape would be cut short. Luckily, there was one person I knew I could still trust. The line trilled as I waited for my brother to pick up.

"Hey, what's going on?" Sam's groggy voice betrayed he'd been asleep.

"Sam, I fucked up bad. Someone dangerous is after you. I'm sorry, but I need your help if there's any chance of us getting out alive." The words rushed from my lips. He had to know how badly I needed him here.

"Hold up. What are you talking about?" The sleepiness disappeared from his voice, replaced by slight suspicion and plenty of concern.

I'm sure part of him suspected what I did, but I never intended to hurt him or drag him into this mess. Yet despite my best intentions, we were caught up in this together, and I hated myself for it. *Save it. Get him here, get out alive, and kick yourself later.* The adrenaline pumping through my veins dulled the pain but did little to help the soreness of every step.

"Sam, I—"

We froze as the mansion's alarm blared in the distance.

"Tim? What's that noise, Tim? Where are you?" His voice was barely audible over the alarm and my beating heart as I struggled to keep moving with Letizia.

I gave him directions on how to get to a road beyond the small forest at the back of the mansion over the loud alarms.

Out of the corner of my eye, I saw dark shadows leave the building through the back, fanning out into search parties. "Shite. Sam, I need you here now. Remember that job I did? It bit me in the ass. I helped the Prosdocimi family. The mobsters, all right? Bring your rifle, please. They know where you live. Just be safe, okay?" One of the guard's flashlights illuminated a patch of grass a few feet away from us, and I hung up. My brother knew where we were. I only hoped he found us in time.

The crack of a snapping twig came from the other side of a tree. I gave Letizia a brief glance. She was pressed low against the tree trunk, her eyes wide. Placing my arms around her, I gathered my strength as I gave her a quick kiss, then leapt into action.

My muscles protested as I took support from the tree and kicked the guard in the groin. The surprise and sudden pain drew little more than a high-pitched squeak. My fist followed soon after with a jab to the face. Stunned but not unconscious, the man reached for his gun. *If he pulls the trigger, everyone will know where we are.* Fear sped up my reactions, and I slammed my elbow into the man's throat.

An audible crunch sickened my stomach as my elbow crushed his windpipe. The guard's eyes bulged as his hands went to his throat, trying to release the pressure closing his airway. Weak and tired, I kicked his gun further away and continued pressing the man against the ground with my weight. His struggles became increasingly more frantic but weaker, until the sudden tensing of his body and a jolt of momentum signaled his final, desperate push for air. And then...nothing.

I slumped against the tree, staring at what I'd done. Emptiness hollowed out my chest. This wasn't what I wanted. I didn't want to kill. Sadly, if I hadn't struck first, he wouldn't have felt the same regret in killing us. Drawing in a deep breath, I climbed to my feet and pulled him out of sight. My muscles were on fire. Adrenaline and survival instincts were all that kept me going, but I was still weak. Eventually the crash would come, and I'd be practically useless.

Letizia had grabbed his gun, which had lain a few feet away in the wet grass. She placed a hand over her mouth as she stared at the body in horror. I pulled her against my chest, needing her touch more than anything else right now. With one of their guards gone, they'd eventually realize he was missing and track where he'd been searching. We leaned against the thick tree and held one another as we tried to recover from the journey out of the mansion.

After several more minutes of searching, the rest of the guards headed back to the mansion's grounds. The men spoke to one another in hushed voices, then the head of the family himself stepped into view.

The mansion's garden lights shone brightly enough to showcase Alonzo as he openly wore the artifact. The two halves of it were merged perfectly together. The pieces hung from a leather cord directly against his chest. Even from this distance, I could see the impact it had on his skin. All around where the amulet touched, the color was drained from his skin. His eyes were now sunken and rimmed with dark circles, but a light burned within his gaze that I'd never seen before. A twinkle of madness mixed with something alien, as if he was no longer in control of himself.

Within moments of the search party gathering, they noticed one of their men was missing. The group of nine armed men headed our way. What I'd give to have my bow. At this distance, the silent weapon would've been near perfect in the evening gloom. Instead, we had a pistol and a knife Letizia had found tucked inside the guard's boot. Better than nothing, but I didn't like our odds one bit.

"Letizia," I whispered, "you need to move deeper into the forest. I don't want them to hurt you. If you stay here, I'll need to focus on keeping you safe and taking them out."

"But I can help you. I know how to fight."

I frowned. "Please, don't make this harder. If they find you with me, I don't think you'll be shown leniency. Your father's different." The footsteps crunched leaves nearby, and I knew we didn't have much time left. "Let me have the knife. It'll be better than the gun. Do you know how to use that?" I pointed to the pistol in her hand. At her nod, I sighed in relief. "Only use it if you need to. Now please, go hide."

"Don't you dare die." She pressed a hard kiss to my lips. It hurt, but I savored every second, then she handed me the knife and snuck deeper into the dark mass of trees.

I leaned my head back against the tree and barely stifled a sigh of relief. The fewer chances of a stray bullet hitting her, the better.

The nine guards took their time approaching. Each man kept his arc of fire away from the rest of the group. It was easy to see they'd done this before. I gripped the knife in my hand, ready to attack when a sudden bark of gunfire went off in the night. The closest guard dropped to the ground unmoving. The guard who stood to his right yelled in alarm, but soon enough, he fell, too.

My eyebrows drew together. When I gave Letizia the gun, this wasn't what I'd had in mind. I'd meant for her to use it if she was in serious danger, but her aim was impressive. However, the guards appeared to be zeroing in on her location.

Another guard dropped near me as he stalked past

where I crouched. It gave me access to his gun, even though I hated firearms. Now, I had no hesitation in using one, especially when it meant keeping us safe.

I squeezed the trigger once, then changed targets before the first man even registered he'd been shot. My aim wasn't quite as sound as Letizia's, but I managed two more shots before their angry replies peppered the tree hiding me. At least most of them were paying attention to me now. Maybe they thought that whoever shot the first two guards had moved.

I'd wounded one guard and downed another. If more men circled around, we'd lose all chance of survival. Moving slowly, I let the trees hide my presence. Once I made it to my new location, I'd be able to fire off another shot or two before they realigned.

Movement to my right stopped me in my tracks. One of the guards was pushing toward Letizia's position. I toyed with the idea of heading him off, but it soon became evident his path would cross with mine. I tucked the gun in my waistband, then pulled out the knife. I dimmed the blade's sheen in the mud and waited. His boots squelched in the muck, betraying his location. My legs wobbled beneath me, ready to send me crashing to the ground, but I held myself up, supported by the tree and waited to see his outline. My calf muscle began to spasm, but I refused to move. The pain kept my senses sharp.

The guard let out a soft yelp as I collided with him. This close, his weapon was useless. A couple quick jabs to his jugular brought him down before he could cry out for help. One moment he'd been closing in on his enemy, the next his eyes held a question about what had happened. I removed the submachine gun he carried and turned toward the path they were approaching en masse.

*Six kills, one wounded. Three at full capacity. Four counting Alonzo.*

But he never moved from his position near the garden's gate. Instead, he watched the activities like a bloodthirsty spectator at the Coliseum. All the while, more color drained from his skin. A wicked grin occasionally played on his features that was nothing like anything he'd done before.

I turned my focus away from him. My mind sought out shapes or movement in the dark, but my surroundings had gone eerily quiet. The momentary distraction benefitted the search party. I'd lost track of them. A sudden *thwack* came a few feet away from where I'd initially been hiding. At first, the pain didn't register, but a few seconds later, a white-hot, searing agony burned my right leg, dropping me to the ground.

The search party rounded the tree close by looking for my body, itching to put a bullet in me. Gunfire burst from the darkness, and two of the guards dropped quickly. Another ducked for cover beside me, nearly tripping over my wounded leg. I aimed the gun at his head and shot him before he could beg for mercy.

Light shone between the tree trunks, too bright for me to see who else was coming. Most likely reinforcements. I switched to the submachine gun and squeezed the trigger, bringing down the first three shapes I saw. The gun kicked and let out a muted sound as it sent each bullet from the barrel.

My right leg ached terribly, but I tried not to pay it much attention as the last of the reinforcements fell. No other movement came from between the trees. I dragged myself backward along the ground, gaining distance from where the guards had last seen me. When I was far enough away, I took a cursory glance at my leg.

The entry wound bled steadily, but it could've been much worse. I hoped the bullet had gone clean through the limb. Tilting my leg to the side made me queasy, but I had to know the extent of the damage. The exit wound was significantly larger. While it missed the arteries and bone itself, it cut right through the muscle. I had to do something about this, or I'd bleed out.

The ground below me was pooling with my blood. I glanced into the forest, knowing our method of escape would come from that way, but moving my leg was sheer agony. Even walking would likely leave a trail of blood behind that could be followed, but I had bigger worries than that.

Two lights shone through the trees, and I lifted my hand to shield my eyes. They were brighter than flashlights. It took a moment to hit me that those couldn't be guards. The soft rumbling of a small car's engine confirmed my suspicions, and I let hope take root that it was my brother.

A gentle hand touched my shoulder, nearly startling me, but Letizia brushed a kiss to my lips. "You should've hidden better. I was repositioning to get a better shot." Concern roughed her voice, and she let her gaze drop to the wound. Her face paled a ghostly white. "It looks really bad. Do you have any other wounds? Sorry, silly question." A frown tightened her lips, but her gaze slid over me methodically as if searching for more severe injuries.

"You shouldn't have brought attention to yourself. That's not what I gave you the gun for." But I couldn't be upset. If it wasn't for her help, I don't know how I could've held out on my own. "But thank you. You're one helluva shot. This is the only gunshot wound." I unfastened my belt and pulled it free from my pants. "More men are likely still out there. Can you help me?" I asked her quietly, and glanced back at the mansion. It took a moment, but she tightened the belt around my leg in a makeshift tourniquet. I wouldn't bleed out there and then, but if I didn't get medical attention soon, I was as good as dead.

"You better thank me, mister. As for my aim, it's the benefit of being raised by a mob boss." She glanced behind us again. "I think I saw a car pull up to the road just behind the forest. It's not too far. If luck is on our side, your brother will be there," Letizia said, holding out her hand. "You're not going to die out here. Let's go."

The headlights had likely attracted the guards' attention. As it was, more flunkies were likely on their way here now. If we had any chance of getting out, it would be in that car.

## 14

## LETIZIA

Timothy was still bleeding, but the tourniquet on his leg seemed to help some. This wasn't my first experience with first aid. I'd helped with some of my family's wounded in the past. He needed to be seen by a medical professional and soon.

The adrenaline pulsing through me waned as the horror of what was happening struck. My father didn't care what happened to me anymore. He had to know I'd helped Timothy escape, and still his men were closing in on the forest road, taking the occasional shot at us.

The car was nowhere to be found, but an unlocked utility shack next to the road gave us somewhere to take shelter. The stone walls wouldn't be easily penetrated by the bullets. Even so, shots chipped away at the building.

We sat beside one another, facing the door watching and waiting for the men to throw it open. Where was Timothy's brother? It was only a matter of time before we both died. Who knew what my father would do to me? And if Timothy didn't get to a hospital, he'd bleed out.

How could my own family do this to us, to me even?

Everything had taken a wrong turn when that damned amulet was found. I wished I could blame it on Timothy for bringing it into my home, but he'd only done his job. It wasn't his fault or my father's. Somehow, the item itself was to blame. Now my father wore it against his skin, uncaring of what went on.

"Are you okay, Letizia?" Timothy asked, not taking his eyes from the building's entrance.

Tears welled up in my eyes. My arms burned, my hands were bruised, and I was exhausted. And yet, he sat here bleeding because I'd wanted to know the man who'd saved me better, and he was asking if I was okay? I licked my lower lip, trying to hold back my emotions.

"I'm okay. I should be the one asking you that instead."

He squeezed my hand. "I'm with you. Of course I'm good." He held up a finger, and silence descended upon the shack again.

The wind whistled through the crack beneath the door, lazily blowing wisps of fog inside. Shadows and the sweep of flashlights moved beyond the aluminum door. The whispered commands coming from around the shack made my stomach feel queasy.

A shadow darkened the space below the door. The doorknob turned slowly as if trying to catch us unaware. Panic built within my chest, and I pressed my hand against my mouth to hold back a whimper.

Timothy lifted his gun.

When the door opened, the guard stared blankly at us, as if he wasn't entirely there. If this were a horror movie, it might've made me think about zombies. A bullet had ripped through his face near his nose. I'd shot him myself. How could he possibly be walking around?

Two shots echoed off the shack's stone walls, then three

more as Timothy kept shooting the guard who just kept coming. Our backs were pressed against the wall behind us, and this...zombie...blocked the door. We had nowhere to run even if we wanted to. With a gentle touch on my leg, Timothy managed to strip away the worst of my fear. How was he not afraid?

Instead of wasting more bullets, Timothy rose to his feet. He wielded the knife expertly, waiting for the right moment to strike the guard down. Watching the two of them made my heart race. Mud and blood coated the guard, causing a grapple from Timothy to slip away. The guard's skin was unnaturally pale, and his eyes were as black as night.

With slow, jerky motions, he lurched toward us with an unwavering certainty. Timothy jabbed the knife through the man's skull near his temple, then removed the blade and stabbed a couple more times.

My stomach churned at the grisly sight, and for a moment, I feared it might not be enough. But the relentless progression stopped, and the body fell backward to the ground. An eerie, chilling cry erupted from the body as black smoke poured from the dead guard's mouth and flew back toward the mansion.

"What was that?" I asked Timothy, touching him on the arm.

He shook his head. "I'm not sure. This seems to be associated with your father's amulet. I've fought something like this before when I first took the job. I hope whatever it is won't bring another tree under its control." Despite his outward calm, his voice shook with something like fear. "If I die here, do what you can to live. Aim for the head and destroy the brain."

I could feel the importance of his words. He didn't want his corpse to turn against me. But could I do it? Could I kill the man I was falling in love with? I wasn't sure. All emotions left me, and I felt drained and numb.

A new shape closed in on the utility shack. I almost closed my eyes, not wanting to see another zombie. Even as I felt any hope of making it out alive dwindle, Timothy let out an excited yelp.

"Sam! Get over here. I almost shot you, idiot," he whispered.

His brother moved closer to us and leaned against the shack beside Timothy.

Their similar features made it clear they were brothers, but they were definitely different. While Timothy had a handsome, almost boyish look to him, Sam looked serious and almost sad. The way he stared at the two of us raised my hackles. He felt otherworldly, as if he didn't belong on this planet. His brother had been right, though. He almost reminded me of my father with how intensely his eyes stared back at me.

"I heard the gunshots, so I started freaking out and drove away." Sam grimaced. "I couldn't leave you here, though. So, I hopped out of the car and decided to walk back to find you. I sensed something this way, so I came over to see what was going on." His words were casual, but his gaze was glued to the corpse. "What the hell is that thing?"

Before either of us could respond, I heard my father's voice nearby. "Mr. Sands, I've enjoyed your servitude to the family, but it's time to close that deal. You've ruined my daughter. She has rebelled against me and even now plots my death. You will suffer for this transgression, and I'll strip her life away from you before I let you die." My father's voice easily carried in the night. Instead of his usual authoritative tone, he sounded shaken and hollow, as if life no longer held meaning for him.

"It's not him. It might look like him, but it's not." My father would never want to hurt me. I was certain of that. The amulet had wormed its way back into our family and was now ripping us apart. Maybe the old stories were true. This could be revenge from a banished family member. A curse to bring ruin to those who betrayed her generations ago. Or maybe it was even older than that? I didn't care anymore.

Shots hit the sides of the shack as my father ordered his men to fire. A pitch-black shadow ducked between the trees near us, as if searching for another corpse to inhabit. The longer I stared at it, the more it looked like it had a demonic shape, but it kept twisting in and out of a clear line of sight. But maybe my eyes were trying to display what I wanted to see.

"What is that?" Sam pointed at the shadow figure, and his gaze seemed to track the being with ease. "I've felt it skulking around, but I've never been this close to something like it. It's—" In his amazement, he started to stand, but Timothy grabbed his arm seconds before a bullet smacked into the wall right above Sam.

We retreated inside the small utility building again where we huddled against the more protected wall to the side of the open door.

A guard crept into view with a grenade in his hand. Before the man could roll it through the door, Timothy fired into his arm and then his leg. The man dropped the grenade, and then fell. He looked around for a moment as if trying to locate the explosive. The horrifying realization on his face came seconds before a muffled explosion shredded through his chest.

I pressed both hands against my mouth, unable to believe what I'd just seen. All I wanted was for this night to be over with. But how would I ever erase these horrible memories from my mind?

Timothy wrapped an arm around my shoulders, bringing me close. "Sshh, sshh. It'll be okay." Even as he spoke, he froze up. The shadow figure headed straight for the smoldering corpse. What use would the shade have with someone so mutilated already? Then again, maybe the man's brain hadn't been injured by the blast.

The moment it touched the guard's charred flesh, an eerie sensation rushed over me, as if a candle had been blown out and was replaced by something black and sulfuric. The corpse rose, and the gunshots paused. The undead turned toward us and took a few quick steps closer. It pulled out another grenade from its pouch. A wide smile spread across its shredded lips, the shadow of a dark entity laid on top of the guard's charred features, grinning in victory.

The zombie's flesh knitted together and then tore. A mass of some kind was growing inside of it, morphing the corpse into an abomination. Whatever the shade had done to the zombies was apparently just a show of its talents. With its enlarged, growing head and razor-sharp fangs, this new horror no longer resembled a human. It blocked our escape from the utility shack, slowly cornering us.

Sam snapped out of it first, firing a shot at the creature as it fumbled with another grenade. It stalked toward us. The impact from the shot didn't seem to make a difference. Sam dropped the rifle. "What are we going to do?"

"Shite. We have to get out of here." Timothy rose to his feet. He turned to look at me. "You said it before. He sounds like your father, but that isn't him anymore. We need to take him down...and soon." Pain ached within his words as if he knew hearing that hurt, but he was right.

Whatever possessed my father wasn't him. Something

had wormed its way into his soul and hollowed him out. His body was merely a shell of who he used to be. Now it was a host to something other. "I know. But we need to get past that thing first," I said, motioning to the lumbering muscle heading our way.

The brothers shared a long look as if unsure what to do. Timothy wouldn't get far in his current state, but we needed some distance from that thing.

When it neared the door, the undead froze in place suddenly.

Sam held out his hand, and sweat dripped down his face. "That's right. I remember what this is now," he muttered.

The corpse lifted its leg as it tried to take another frustrated step. Each movement was slow and jerky, as if it moved through water or maybe even molasses.

Timothy didn't hesitate. He fired another shot straight into the undead's head.

The victorious grin on the demon's face twisted with anger. The corpse's mouth moved, but no sound escaped.

"What did you do, Sam?" Timothy's surprise and fear were evident in his voice.

"I don't know." Sam hesitated for a moment. "But I've done this before." He lowered his hand to the ground below. "Take care of my brother. If you don't, I'll come back to haunt you." Sam stared at me. No humor existed in his voice, and his eyes were black voids. He moved toward the door, blocking the corpse from coming closer but leaving us enough space to run.

I supported Timothy as we hurried toward Sam's car, but he kept glancing back.

"Sam! Hurry up! Sam," he yelled. "We need to leave."

As we approached our getaway car, I spotted my father leaning against it.

The shade zipped through the scenery and dove back into my father's skin. Deep black lines stretched across his features. Somehow, that monster was feeding off him. Like a leech, it absorbed his life force to keep doing what it wanted. After a moment, my father gasped, nearly falling to his knees.

"Are you coming to beg for mercy from your father, Letizia? That's too bad. I've almost devoured him whole. Don't worry. You will be next in line as a fitting dessert to my ambition." A hollow, inhuman voice came from my father. His eyes were now entirely black as he slowly stumbled toward us. His now white skin nearly glowed in the moonlight, marred only by pulsing, obsidian veins.

My poor father didn't have long. Anger rose within my chest, then pity and sorrow as I took another look at my father. He reminded me more of the hulking monstrosity behind us than the vigorous man he'd been just days ago.

As my father neared, I lifted my pistol to put him out of his misery, but my hands and arms trembled. Even at this range, I wasn't sure I'd be successful. Sighing, I lowered the gun once more.

Timothy fired three shots at my father, moving forward a little to protect me.

"Oh, my poor girl, what have they done to you? Unable to stand up for yourself." The voice mocked everything Papa stood for. If it tried to make me feel bad, it didn't know me at all. I'd heard worse things in my life, and I knew that wasn't my father. It was evil. Trash to be taken out.

My tears could wait. For now, we needed to survive. I lifted my arms again and fired a shot at my father, striking him in the chest.

Where the shots connected, the body simply shook from the impact. Wounds formed, but no blood came out. Had that thing drained my father dry?

Timothy cursed under his breath. "Bloody hell…"

The thing possessing my father smiled, but I didn't notice why until it was too late.

We were surrounded.

A zombie—in process of going through the same mutation as the horror we'd left with Sam—made a grab for me but missed.

"Now, now. Be a good little puppet, Alonzo, and I might keep your daughter alive for a bit longer." Papa's face twitched as if he battled with the demon within him. "Don't worry. I'll make sure you listen to her screams as I make you do what I want for as long as I want. Oh, the misery we'll inflict. It will be wonderful." The voice coming from my father laughed at me, sending a chill down my spine.

He was still in there? What should we do?

"Leave my father alone!" I yelled and backed away from the zombie still coming at me.

The creature reached for me again, but my father grabbed it. "Don't harm my daughter." Papa's voice came through, then the creepy voice added, "I need her alive."

The interaction gave me a chance to run on the slippery ground.

"If you want to keep your brother alive, drop the gun," my father croaked as the lumbering monstrosity walked toward us, clutching Sam in its oversized arm that looked as if eels had erupted from its hand. The pulsating tentacles circled Sam's head.

"No!" I tore my gaze away from the scene.

Timothy froze beside me. He looked between me and Sam. "We have to do something. He's my brother."

My father cackled and rose upright. "Ah! It's so good to see a family brought back together." He chuckled as the monster brought Sam closer.

From the edge of the forest, I saw bodies twitching and slowly rising back up. Whatever unholy power the being had worked to reanimate the corpses again. "Come, daughter. Join us willingly, and I'll let them live long, painful lives serving us," my father said as he collapsed. His body was almost entirely covered in black veins. His muscles appeared to shrivel before my eyes, being absorbed by the thing feeding off him.

"Hey, catch!"

A shout nearby seemed not to fit the moment, and it caught me entirely off-guard. It almost sounded like Sam, but that didn't make any sense. A small, round object clattered next to my father, and I leapt for cover as the grenade went off.

Timothy kept shooting at a zombie near me, even as I grabbed my gun.

Sam screamed at the top of his lungs, but my primary focus was on ending this. I ran past the zombie and grabbed the knife from Timothy. My legs kicked up dirt as I sprinted for my father.

Big holes dotted his head, chest, and neck, but my father still stood. His glare was cold with hatred. He cursed at me in a guttural language I didn't recognize.

"Be quiet!" I snapped and shoved the blade into my father's chest, then I slashed the knife into the amulet. A quick punch to my chest threw me off-balance. Air burst from my lungs. I struggled to climb back to my feet. My father inched closer, his arms reaching for my neck.

Timothy slammed into him, knocking my father to the grass.

I crawled toward my father. All sense of self-preservation was gone. We had to end this.

It hurt to draw breath, but I pulled myself over my father's body.

"Let go of him!" I wasn't sure if it understood me anymore, but I speared it with one last hateful glare and wrenched the amulet apart with the knife.

Papa's eyes fluttered opened. "Letizia?" Air wheezed from his throat. "My beautiful girl, is...is that you?" His hand weakly lifted to touch my face, but it dropped back to the ground. "I'm so sorry...for everything."

Tears blurred my vision, and emotion tightened my throat. "It's okay, Papa. I love you. We'll get help. Just stay with us." But I could already see the life fading from his eyes.

## 15

# TIMOTHY

"Miss Letizia? Bella, are you okay?" The man's careful voice sounded like one of Alonzo's staff instead of any guard I'd met.

I knelt by Letizia's side, gently hugging her to my chest. Neither of us responded. My gaze fixed on Sam who was rocking himself beside the dead, tentacled monster. Part of me wondered if this was a trap. Was the family here to finish us off?

"Mario?" she said.

"Yes, bella. Come out, please. You're safe. No one will hurt you." Mario's footsteps closed in on our location, and he came into view. At the sight of Alonzo's body, he gasped in horror.

Letizia lifted her gaze to mine. She looked exhausted and wary, but a stony resolution straightened her posture, transforming her back into the woman I'd known before this. "I'll come back to the house. Both myself and my lover are armed, so if you try anything, I will shoot."

"No weapons are out here. All we want to do is take care

of you and make sure you're safe." He cleared his throat, his gaze sliding over us. "We can help your lover, too."

Slowly, I rose to my feet to make sure Mario was telling the truth. Now I could see what else the man had found. This place looked like the scene of a massacre. Limbs had been torn from the guards. The bodies ashen white and seemingly drained of blood.

Letizia took my hand and stood with me. She looked at her father's body with sorrow, but it spoke to me more than words could have. A smile of peace was on his lips, and the artifact lay broken in several pieces against his bare chest. Where it had pressed against him, the skin was still pale with blackened veins that spread outward across his entire body.

I walked back to toward my brother, giving Letizia the chance to say goodbye to her father in private. He was in the same spot as before and just as unmoving. "Hey, Sam? Are you okay?"

A distant look haunted his eyes. He rocked himself faster, blankly staring at the trees. "What am I?" The hushed question was like a slap in the face. "What am I, Timothy?" His body slumped, and he closed his eyes, collapsing to the ground.

After checking his pulse and seeing if he had any serious wounds, I doubted my brother was in any immediate danger. Maybe he'd fainted. Bloody hell... The more I moved, the less energy I had. If I didn't seek medical attention soon, Alonzo's wish to not have me with his daughter might be fulfilled.

"Timothy?" Letizia's voice drew my attention. A tall man with white hair stood beside her. "We should get back to the mansion. I spoke with the doctor," she said, waving to the man, "about your injuries. He's going to take care of you." Her gaze drifted to Sam. "Is your brother okay?" She waved for someone out of view. Two guards approached. They lifted my brother and carried him in the mansion's direction while Letizia supported me as we traveled together.

It was eerie returning to the place I'd so desperately fled. Once we made it back, the mood was sullen. However, the air inside the mansion had cleared like the refreshing scent of rain after a storm. But what had we won here? And at what cost?

Letizia could spend her life with me, but her father and several others who had been loyal to her family were now dead. Was my life worth all that loss?

My legs nearly gave out on the bottom step, taking Letizia with me. The bleeding wound made it hard to focus on anything, but there were two things I valued: my brother and Letizia. While I didn't know what was going on with Sam, I couldn't help but feel indebted to him. He'd saved me and my love. How could I ever repay him? But I'd do what I needed to keep him in my life. It was my turn to keep him safe.

Once the doctor was finished patching me up, Letizia and I curled up on her bed together. He suspected I had a few broken ribs from the beating. Those would be fully explored later. At least the bullet had gone clean through. It would take time to fully heal, but with Letizia at my side, I held hope for the future, regardless of how dark life seemed now.

"How are you feeling?" Letizia asked.

"I think I should be asking you that." I stretched my arm out, inviting her closer. "I've been beaten up and shot at, but there's no one else I'd rather share my life with than you." These words weren't easy for me, but I cleared my throat.

"Whatever happens, we can get through it together, if you want. I love you, Letizia."

Her lips parted, and she smacked me on the chest. Pain shot through my battered body, and I winced. "Oops! I'm sorry. It's just..." She snuggled closer. "That's the first time anyone other than my parents have said that. Are you sure you do?"

"Quite sure. Although, if you keep hitting—"

She brushed her soft lips against mine. That simple gesture stole away the agony clenching at me better than the doctor's painkillers. "I love you, too, Timothy. I really do. Life probably won't be stress-free, but knowing I have someone to share the good and bad with makes this evening slightly easier to handle. So much life was lost...for nothing."

"Whatever you need, know that I'm here for you."

We snuggled closer together, falling asleep in one another's arms as the exhaustion of the evening's events and injuries finally took hold.

———

LIFE WAS different since Alonzo Prosdocimi's death. It had taken a while to recover from my wounds, but the family had remained true to their word when they offered to help me. Any remaining debt I'd had was forgiven. Although, I suspected my relationship with Letizia played a role in that.

Other things had changed, too.

Letizia admitted to the family that she'd never wanted to play a large role in the family's unsavory side. While she was fine with helping to run the family's legal businesses, the thought of playing a role in the criminal underworld didn't appeal to her. Instead, her cousin Roberto had been designated as the head of the family. Although, I suspected that Letizia would still help run the numbers. She didn't seem too confident in her cousin's capability of handling it all himself.

My time was spent helping Letizia with both the legal and illegal side of her family's business, except this time I held a role of authority. No more did I have to worry about losing my head for not doing exactly what was expected on someone else's timeline. More importantly, I didn't need to fear for my life just because I loved Letizia, and I appreciated that more than anything since she always knew how to make me laugh and feel loved.

My first order had been to send Little Boy away to find new recruits for the family. As much as I loathed the man, he was loyal to the family and would do well with training newbies. Besides, it kept him occupied and away from the mansion.

Sam still wasn't doing well since that fateful night. His mental condition had continually deteriorated until he barely functioned now. I hated seeing him waste away like that, and time would come when I'd need to make a decision for him.

"Mr. Sands?" Mario said, drawing my attention to the library's door.

"Yes?"

"There's a guest for you here." He paused for a moment with a frown on his lips. "He says you're expecting him?"

That couldn't be right. Who would think to look for me here? The only people who knew my location were my brother and the family, and I doubted any of them would necessitate Mario asking me about having an audience with them.

"Sure, send him in."

I raised my eyebrows as the strange man from outside the museum appeared in the doorway. I'd never caught his name. The way he moved as he got closer made me nervous. From his pacing, I could tell he'd been here before, but this time, he didn't bother displaying his guns.

"Timothy, I see you've managed to pull through the situation. Not the way I would've done, but nevertheless, it is impressive to see you are still alive. Doubly so with the amount of stupid and reckless decisions you made in order to get here. Regardless, I do believe congratulations are in order. You are, after all, now part of the few remaining families operating in London that are not currently under investigation by the Crown." The man touched the spines on some of the older books as he made his way to me. His tone was refined, to the point, but not as arrogant as I'd expected. He appeared in complete control, his posture as reserved as it had been at the museum.

"That's interesting. If you knew what took place, why didn't you intervene?" I asked, keeping my nerves calm. "I suspect my brother would be in much better shape. As it is now, I have little choice other than to send him to an asylum." I snapped shut the book in front of me with more frustration than I'd intended. Keeping my gaze on him, I rose to meet him face to face.

"Ah. I dare say he will be exactly where he'll be needed, Timothy. Perhaps not of his own volition, but people often put too much faith in free will. Alas, he is not the primary reason for my visit. The vessel that housed the entity is now broken. This is a somewhat sensitive subject here. Agencies exist that are highly interested in ensuring other artifacts of a similar nature to what you found are not placed within the wrong hands. Sadly, many of the people who find these items are ill-equipped to handle them appropriately, but you've shown promise in this field. What do you say, Mr. Sands? Would you be interested in using your resources to ensure events like what you and your family experienced do not repeat?" he asked with a slight smile on his lips.

"I'm not sure what you're saying here, sir—"

Before I could say more, the man began to chuckle.

"Oh. Don't worry about that," he said. "So many things lie ahead of us. We merely do our best to tip the scales in our favor." He pulled out a thick, manila envelope and held it out to me. "After all, I put a wager in for you." An easy grin slid over his lips.

I knew that smile.

It was the same one every dealer had on their face as they dealt the cards. The one that, more than anything, made me sweat. Would I rise to the challenge and play my hand or call the bluff? I released a sigh and took the envelope from the mysterious man before me.

*Life's a gamble anyway. But this gambit will be my choice.*

———

**Looking for more fantasy adventures? Grab *Captivated*, a book filled with danger, faeries, and elves, oh my...**

## AUTHOR'S NOTE

Thank you for reading *The Thief's Gambit*. We hope you enjoyed it!

Please consider leaving a review at the retailer's website or on Goodreads, even if it's a line or two. It truly helps!

**If you're interested in being the first to know about our next releases, sign up for Sarah's newsletter.**

# ACKNOWLEDGMENTS

Special thank you to our editor Liz from EB Editorial Services. She's been incredible with her feedback and support of this book.

We'd also like to thank Donna and Linda for beta reading it.

Finally, we'd like to thank our readers for their patience with this book. It's been a long time coming, but it's finally here. Hooray!

# ABOUT SARAH MÄKELÄ

New York Times & USA Today Bestselling Author Sarah Mäkelä loves her fiction dark, magical, and passionate. She is a paranormal romance author and a life-long paranormal fan who still sleeps with a night light. In her spare time, she reads sexy books, watches scary movies, and plays computer games with her husband. When she gets the chance, she loves traveling the world too.

a  amazon.com/author/sarahmakela

BB  bookbub.com/authors/sarah-makela

○  instagram.com/authorsarahmakela

f  facebook.com/authorsarahmakela

🐦  twitter.com/sarahmakela

g  goodreads.com/sarahmakela

P  pinterest.com/authorsarahmakela

## ABOUT TAVIN SØREN

Tavin Søren is an urban fantasy author. He loves whiskey, has a sense of adventure, and enjoys learning about all things supernatural.

# ALSO BY SARAH MÄKELÄ

**The Amazon Chronicles Series**

(New Adult Paranormal Romance)

Book 1: Jungle Heat

Book 2: Jungle Fire

Book 3: Jungle Blaze

Book 4: Jungle Burn

*The Amazon Chronicles Collection*

**Hacked Investigations Series**

(Futuristic Paranormal Romance)

Book 1: Techno Crazed

Book 2: Savage Bytes

Book 2.5: Internet Dating for Gnomes *

Book 3: Blacklist Rogue

Book 4: Digital Slave

**Courts of Light and Dark**

(New Adult Fantasy Romance)

Book 1: Captivated

Book 2: Surrendered

**Standalones**

Moonlit Feathers

Captive Moonlight

Vera's Christmas Elf

## ALSO BY TAVIN SØREN

**Edge of Oblivion**

Book 1: The Assassin's Mark

Book 2: The Thief's Gambit

# EXCERPT FOR CAPTIVATED

Gritting her teeth, Honora Butler sneaked farther into the dark, snowy forest. Danger lurked within the shadows, and she would kill or be killed. Death didn't intimidate her anymore. She knew it too well.

Everyone she'd loved had been taken from her. The only thing she cared about now was destroying those who had ruined her life.

Snow crunched beneath the soles of her knee-high leather boots. The risks of killing those monsters were great, but she didn't care. When she was young, the Mercenary Guild had taken her in. They'd seen her abilities and her determination. They'd trained her, given her a chance when she'd wanted only to die, and now she did what she bloody well could to make sure the dark beings of the Unseelie Court hurt no one else.

A horrified scream erupted ahead, beckoning her deeper into the forest. It had to have been caused by her prey. Picking up her pace, she pulled a throwing knife from its sheath. Her magic surged into the blade, filling it with power and making the metal white-hot.

The trees broke into a clearing. The cause of the cries stood in the dirt road. A woman cowered on the ground while a short, stocky man dressed in blood red with a matching hat sneered at her. He looked to be having far too good a time.

"I have a husband and kids. Please, don't hurt me," the woman whimpered. "My master...he'll—"

The Fear Dearg snorted and crossed his arms in front of him. Stroking his bushy beard, he stared down his crooked nose at the terrified woman as if pondering what to do first.

Honora doubted the woman was in immediate danger. The Red Man mostly engaged in cruel pranks on those he sought, but that wouldn't stop her from killing him. Her mission in life was to rid the world of malevolence. No matter what.

She slid from the trees, taking one quiet step after another. "*Na dean maggadh fum,*" she said. Those words, '*Do not mock me,*' were the best chance she had to take him down without a problem.

The Fear Dearg jerked his gaze to Honora. His lips curled back into a snarl at the interruption. "So be it. Now go on. Get out of here. Can't you see I'm busy?" He stared at her blankly, waiting. "What? You want my favor and prosperity? One of those bold adventurers? Wait for your turn."

Just like that, he returned his focus to the woman, grabbing for her dress.

With a snap of her wrist, Honora sent the throwing knife sailing through the air. A wash of blood arced in a thick spray as the Fear Dearg collapsed, the knife lodged between his eyes.

Shrieking, the woman scurried backwards from the corpse. Her eyes were wide and horrified at the sight of the dead faerie. "What have you done?" she asked, glancing

Honora's way. Shaking her head, she reached for her large basket with foodstuffs that lay on its side. Most of the food had fallen out, but the woman didn't bother gathering it. She just took the basket, then ran off down the dirt road.

What had that been about?

Honora watched the woman until she disappeared around the curve of the path. She walked over to the dead Red Man, then tugged her blade out of his skull. It came away easily, blood dripping off it in great crimson drops. She wiped it clean on his jacket before tucking the knife back in its sheath.

Her stomach rumbled. On the ground was an unsoiled loaf of bread from the woman's fallen food. She stripped off her bloody gloves and crouched. After brushing off a few leaves, she tore a piece from it and lifted it to her lips.

In the distance, she heard a faint noise like that of a large flock of birds beating their wings. That couldn't be right. Birds weren't typically active at night there. Yet the sound grew louder.

The sudden realization of what it was punched her in the gut. She dropped the bread and raced after the woman. Honora needed to find the safety of shelter. She couldn't be out here when the Sluagh—restless spirits of the dead—flew over. What they did was worse than death. They captured their victims' souls.

Behind her, the cries became impossibly louder. She didn't have much time at all. She had yet to spot any homes or places to hide and knew if she were spotted, she would be connected with the murder of the Fear Dearg. They'd hunt her down. She wouldn't be safe unless she found somewhere soon.

Chancing a look over her shoulder, she saw a horrible black mass darken the sky. Screams of their victims filled her ears. They were close. She caught sight of an elegant manor off to the left.

She sprinted, pushing herself to pick up her speed. Her legs ached with the strain, but she refused to slow down. Not with the dark creatures flying behind her, closing in despite each step she took.

Within a few tiring moments, Honora reached the massive wooden door. She knocked hard, and when there was no response, she pushed against it. The door opened easily.

Her ears hurt from the screeching noise. She pressed her back against the door as a heavy force slammed into it, nearly throwing her to the floor.

Honora's gaze drifted over the opulence surrounding her. Shite. She didn't want to be here long. Who knew whom this place belonged to? She twisted around to face the door, then slammed the lock in place. Whoever it was didn't seem familiar with locking their door. Leaning against the solid wood, she heard the Sluagh circling the manor, searching for a weakness.

For whatever reason, they retreated. Uneasiness flared within her—they weren't known to do that. Maybe they'd found another victim. No, she found that hard to believe. The other option was that they recognized whoever's place she'd entered. That didn't bode well, did it?